The Silver Riders

Greg Hatcher

AIRSHIP 27 PRODUCTIONS

The Silver Riders
© 2017 Greg Hatcher

DEDICATION
*For the memory of the real Anne-Marie,
and all of us who loved her.*

Published by Airship 27 Productions
www.airship27.com
www.airship27hangar.com

Interior illustrations © 2017 Chris Kohler
Cover illustration © 2017 Adam Shaw

Editor: Ron Fortier
Associate Editor: Jay Sweet
Marketing and Promotions Manager: Michael Vance
Production and design by Rob Davis.

ISBN-13: 978-1-946183-29-3
ISBN-10: 1-946183-29-6

Printed in the United States of America

10 9 8 7 6 5 4 3 2 1

Man's law changes with his understanding of man.
Only the laws of the spirit remain always the same.

—proverb of the Crow tribe

…I stood atop the ancient crumbling wall
And strained to hear the trumpet call
I leaned a bit too far and lost my hold

I fell into the unforgiving sand
Barely missed the saving hand
And I was crushed beneath the falling wall

Can you hear my heart beat?
Over the walls falling
Walls falling on me?
Listen to my heart beat

Let the cold wind blow
Rough night in Jericho
Let the walls fall in
Guess I'll be saved by love again
Rough night in Jericho

Even though the walls are falling
I swear I hear the calling now

■ "Rough Night In Jericho," Barry Marler

One
Silver & Black

Cheyanne Parsons looked up from the ledger she had spread before her on the rough-cut pine table and glared at the injured logger seated across from her. "Lucas, you got to lay off that moaning. Doctor Lisbet will be back well before sundown, I promise. It's just the Svensons and their colicky baby that she has to look in on."

The unfortunate logger looked back at her, his eyes woeful and a little frightened. "But it *hurts*, Cheyanne. And this morning it started smellin. I don't want Doctor Lisbet to have to saw it off. I knew a fella down in Shelby what had to lop his whole leg off just above the knee and that was just a bug bite or something."

He shifted on the upended crate he was sitting on and started to reach for his own knee, which was poking out through a hole in the denim pantleg to display an ugly four-inch tear in the flesh. The skin around the tear was bright red with inflammation and the wound itself was black around the edges and oozing. The skin was laid open a little, and the tissue looked yellow and spongy underneath.

Cheyanne snapped at him. "Don't keep touching it with your great filthy hands! You'll get dirt in there and then it *will* get infected! You are being worse than the Svenson baby, I swear." Lucas looked so crestfallen at this that she added softly, "Doctor Lisbet knows what she's doing, Lucas, trust me. You aren't gonna lose the leg."

"Woman doctor ain't natural." This growl was more for dignity's sake than anything, Cheyanne knew. Lucas did trust Doctor Lisbet—everyone in the settlement did. At first it had been grudging, because Elizabeth Shaw, in her fringed leather duster and knitted gray scarf, was the sole option for medical care within a hundred miles of Hackett Creek, and it was a take-it-or-leave-it proposition. But no one understood why the tall Eastern lady with the silver-streaked hair and the big black stallion would want to settle here. Well-spoken ladies from Boston simply did not go to logging camps and build themselves cabins in this Year of Our Lord 1878. Let alone ladies who claimed to be doctors.

But Doctor Lisbet proved herself soon enough, and if her bedside manner was occasionally a bit clipped (Cheyanne thought that the doctor had every right to her impatience, given that most patients were mulishly stubborn about their home remedies despite endless explanations about why it was preferable to treat wounds with alcohol or carbolic instead of weed poultices laced with butter and rose oil)... well, anyway, after a few years the families of Hackett Creek had indeed come to trust Doctor Lisbet despite her eccentricities.

But they feared her a little, too. Even today, almost ten years to the day since her arrival.

The unknown always invites speculation, and Doctor Lisbet had remained amiably but relentlessly silent about her own history and her reason for choosing Hackett Creek to set up her practice. Not even a hint. It was known she was from Boston, that she had studied medicine and was a real doctor, and it was obvious from her skill and intelligence that she had done well at her studies. But that was all. No one knew what drove her to leave Boston and come here to the Oregon Territory. *Fine lady like her belongs someplace like San Francisco,* the locals opined with puzzled looks. What could be in Hackett Creek? Hardly anyone besides a couple of mill owners downriver even knew the camp existed.

She's hiding, likely, people whispered. *Must be a man. It's always a man.*

It could have been something like that, Cheyanne supposed. But Lisbet never discussed it and people rarely asked her straight out. Though she was good-humored with everyone most of the time, there was a quality of reserve about the doctor, a sort of psychic boundary she kept around herself that most feared to cross. The severity of her temper, once unleashed, was a fearsome thing. Few had seen it besides Cheyanne, like for instance when she and Doctor Lisbet had come upon two of the Wilson boys tormenting a wolf caught in some mountain man's ancient and forgotten bear trap. She had not laid a hand on them but her words were so harsh and contemptuous Cheyanne would have privately wagered that there were still visible stripes produced on their vicious little backsides when she had finally sent them off with a warning that their parents would hear of their laughter at the suffering of a helpless animal. Then she and Cheyanne had freed the wolf, and Cheyanne had marveled at how quiet the beast had been, even letting Doctor Lisbet carry him down the mountain to her office and clean the wound and stitch him up. Cheyanne had heard the doctor whispering to the animal on the way down and when she asked what it was, Lisbet looked a little uncomfortable. "Something you say to animals to ease their pain."

"But it wasn't English."

"Still worked." Lisbet's elegant mouth quirked in a rueful smile, almost as though she hadn't expected results either. She shook her head and then moved forward, dismissing it.

But Cheyanne wasn't done. "Teach me?"

For a moment Cheyanne thought she saw real pain on the doctor's face. "I think it would be better for you to keep up with your regular schoolwork. You have years to pursue side projects."

"But you taught me knitting. Isn't this like that?"

"You just tend to your knitting for now." And that was the end of it.

Cheyanne wondered about it for a while, especially when Lisbet had decreed the animal would sleep in the consulting room. "I gave him a spoonful of laudanum," she said flatly. "Go to bed now and I'll shut him safely in the other room and then we will get settled in ourselves. I will release him in the morning once I'm sure that wound isn't infected."

Cheyanne had just nodded; when Doctor Lisbet took that tone she would brook no objection. But the following morning, she heard the doctor saying more words in the unknown tongue as she released the wolf almost exactly at the sunrise.

There had been no laudanum, and they both knew it.

Cheyanne said nothing. The doctor often took in strays and healed them, the same as with people. Cheyanne didn't care why—she would have done the same herself, and assumed Lisbet had similar feelings. But the *how* of it made her intensely curious.

There had been other little odd moments like that in the nine years Cheyanne had been with the doctor. She was herself a stray, left to fend for herself at the age of six when her mother had died in childbirth on Lisbet's rude operating table. The baby had been stillborn as well, leaving Cheyanne with no family at all in the world as far as she knew. Doctor Lisbet had questioned her closely about the father's whereabouts but Cheyanne truly had no idea; all her mother had ever said was that he was a bad man and they were better alone. Of her own father she knew nothing, save that it seemed her mother had made poor choices with the men in her life. They had always been alone, for the most part. Cheyanne had been looking forward to the baby, and to having a younger sibling she could love and care for as fiercely as her own mother had loved and cared for her. But now she had no one at all.

Except that it turned out she did. Doctor Lisbet had shrugged and accepted the inevitable. There was no one else to take charge of the orphaned girl, and anyway, an extra pair of hands around the place never hurt. Even Cheyanne's young ones.

Cheyanne had been appalled at first. The thought of growing up in the middle of nowhere, alone, with no family around her save for the raven-and-silver-haired doctor lady with the no-nonsense manner and the severe gray eyes, depressed and frightened her. But she adjusted much faster than an adult would have, as children do, and soon Hackett Creek had become her home. She even came to love it with the same kind of impatient affection Doctor Lisbet herself seemed to. The low mountain country of eastern Oregon, the Deschutes forests and all that went with them, was some of the most beautiful country Cheyanne had ever seen, and since Lisbet loved to walk and often took her along when she made doctor's rounds, she had seen a great deal of that country around the camp.

Hackett Creek had little to recommend it other than forest and quiet. There was one saloon that was largely deserted during the week but made it all up Saturday nights when payroll was distributed, a number of traders dealing in tools and other things the loggers couldn't hunt, grow, or build for themselves, and a small schoolhouse and inn, both maintained by the widow Jarvis.

This last concern actually was something the mill owners had arranged amongst themselves as an act of charity when Birdie's late husband, Oswald "Buck" Jarvis, had lost an arm trying to shove one of his colleagues out of the way of a cascade of debris when a flume had burst a joint and sent tons of water and logs flooding into the crew waiting below. Doctor Lisbet had struggled to save him but the man simply had lost too much blood and expired within an hour of the accident. Birdie was a canny freckled lass from the old country, though, and had made the business work, adding a small café to the front of the boardinghouse and tailoring her menu to families and other, non-drunken, customers like travelers too weary to tie one on at the saloon or business men coming in to talk to the mill owners. When the owners noticed her success and were starting to think of genuinely investing further in the venture the widow had surprised everyone and bought *them* out instead, thanking them kindly for their faith in her.

Few knew that the money for the buyout had come in part from Elizabeth Shaw. No one but Birdie Jarvis and Cheyanne knew that the agreement was not that Doctor Lisbet would be repaid in cash eventually, but instead that part of the money would go to a school. "Families need to educate their children," the doctor had said, simply, when Cheyanne came across the agreement while tidying the doctor's papers. "I consider education to be a moral duty."

"I thought kids learned about morals in church."

A shadow flitted across Doctor Lisbet's face. "That has not been my experience. Rather the reverse, if anything."

Cheyanne had been intensely curious about this—in her life she had never met anyone who would dare to suggest that churches were not moral—but, again, it was clearly something Doctor Lisbet did not want to discuss and so she dropped it.

There was a thump of a burden being set down on the planking of the front porch and then Doctor Lisbet bustled in. "Cheyanne, the Svensons presented us with a bag of produce as payment, mostly potatoes. Can you possibly get them into the root cellar while I—well, hello, Lucas." She made a show of sniffing the air. "Good heavens, that leg is going to have to come off—"

Lucas, his expression unutterably tragic, let out another animal groan.

"—that is, if you don't get into my workroom right now and let me clean it out and stitch it up." Doctor Lisbet eyed the logger for a moment and then, satisfied with the effect her words had produced, went on, "Now, I'm going to have to scrape it some as well. It will hurt like hellfire. I can give you something here but you must not medicate yourself with whiskey later when it starts to hurt again. You will open your weakened body up to attack by other diseases if you do, and your whiskey-impaired brain will probably lead to further poor decisions. Why in heaven's name did you wait so long to get this seen to?"

"Just a cut," Lucas said. "Didn't think nothing of it till it started oozing and smellin bad."

Doctor Lisbet shook her head. "Next time you get one that deep you come see me. Don't be such a prideful man about it. All right, come on back. Cheyanne, please, see to the vegetables and get Sultan put away, he's had a hard day too. Difficult trails for a horse, but it was too wet to walk. Anyway, get him into his stall and rub him down a little. You might treat him to some oats, he worked much more than I did."

"Yes'm." Cheyanne nodded and bounded outside.

It was as she was giving Sultan his promised oats that she saw the stranger approaching on the big bay. He dismounted and stared past Cheyanne into the stable.

"Sultan?" he said in a tone of low wonder. "Still? Holy mother of God that's a game horse. Thought he'd be long gone by now." He turned to Cheyanne. "I'm here to see Elizabeth Shaw. They said at the saloon this was her place. Who are you?"

"Who are *you*?" Cheyanne stuck her chin out.

The stranger chuckled and doffed his hat. He was tall, and dressed all in black, from his shirt to his boots. Even his eyes were covered by dark spectacles. His hair was streaked black-and-silver, much like Doctor Lisbet's, and his face was deeply tanned and careworn. She couldn't see his eyes behind the smoked glasses he wore, but his smile was kind. "Fair enough, miss. I'm Jonas Fallon. I'm an old friend of Elizabeth's."

Old... friend? Cheyanne was so stonkered by this that she just stared at the stranger in open-mouthed shock for a moment. "Well—she's with a patient but I'm sure she'll see you. Come inside where it's warm, there's a stove. I'm Cheyanne."

"Thank you kindly, Miss Cheyanne." Fallon clumped up the wooden steps behind Cheyanne, and once inside the cabin, squatted on his haunches in front of the potbelly stove in the front room, warming his hands. "Ah, now that's better," he murmured.

Cheyanne's mind was boiling with questions. *How do you know Doctor Lisbet? How did you know to come here? Is she hiding like everyone says? Are you hiding too? Who is she really? Who are you really?* But what came out was a stuttering, "Would you like some, uh, tea or something?"

"Coffee?"

"We don't keep any here, I'm afraid. But the tea is healthful," she added hopefully. "Doctor Lisbet makes it herself from herbs we grow here."

"Oh, I've no doubt of its healing properties." Fallon stood and looked appraisingly at Cheyanne for a moment. "Lisbet's quite the miracle worker hereabouts, I expect." He paused and added, "You see a lot of ravens in these parts maybe?"

Cheyanne shook her head. "No. Why would you ask something like that?"

"Just curious." Fallon smiled again, but there was something rueful and dark in it. "Ravens are an omen to some."

"Doctor Lisbet doesn't believe in omens. She believes in science, and medicine," Cheyanne said stoutly.

Inexplicably, this made Fallon laugh out loud. "Well good for her," he said. "That eases my thinking quite a bit."

The door to Doctor Lisbet's consulting room opened and Lucas came limping out, looking woebegone. Doctor Lisbet's voice came from the room after him, "Remember about the whiskey, Lucas."

"I'll member." Lucas shuffled out the front door just as Doctor Lisbet herself appeared. She stopped and stared at Fallon.

Fallon smiled. "Hello, gorgeous."

"Oh my God, Jonas," Lisbet choked out. She swept forward and gathered Jonas Fallon in a brief hug. "I thought I was the only one. That you were lost."

The way she said it, Cheyanne knew she meant something like lost at sea or something. Dead.

Fallon shook his head. "Maybe we all been lost for the last ten years," he said. "On purpose. I tried drinking for a while but it didn't help. I'm sure Brainerd found himself some filly. Or a dozen. Aaron got out too, and Larry. Took me some time figuring out where you were. But whatever. I'm here and I need you. All of you."

"I'm done with that." Doctor Lisbet was using her firm voice, the one that usually stopped conversation on a subject.

But this man sailed past it like he didn't even notice. "Yeah? You expect me to believe you didn't use Language on that boy just now?"

"I do expect it, because I did not. I used medical knowledge and skill. And a teaspoon of laudanum," she added wryly. Suddenly she noticed Cheyanne was staring avidly at the both of them. "Come on back into my consulting room, Jonas, and we can talk."

Cheyanne waited until the door closed, and then crept to a position near the jamb where she could listen. The door was stout but badly hung, and their voices could he heard easily through the gap.

Doctor Lisbet sounded as exasperated as she did when a patient was doing something stupid and self-destructive. "Jonas, I don't think I *can* use Language any more. I would be no help to you. And it's a fool's errand to go back there. The abbey burned, it's gone. We were fortunate to escape with our lives. Let it end there."

"But it won't end, Lisbet. You know it won't. Ravens are gathering in the desert. And there are rumors. Guy in Three Forks swore to me he saw a woman who could—"

"Anne-Marie is dead."

"She might not be. We're not."

"She has to be." But Lisbet's voice was unsure.

"If she's not—"

"She *has* to be!" This time it was firm. "Yes, very well, you are probably right. The obsidian likely is awakened. What can we do?" She sighed. "It will take another fifty years to weave itself whole, probably, and we will be long dead by then. Let it go."

"Your little girl out there might still be around to see it. Is that how you want her to end? Her and everyone else?" Fallon's voice was edged and hard. "We owe it to them innocent folks. We did this to 'em. We have to fix it. You were her best friend, without you we got no chance at all. More'n that. We owe Anne-Marie. If it's really her—if'n we can pull her back from the edge—"

"Jonas, be reasonable. We are—look at you. You are as gray as I am." Lisbet's voice was shaky. "That place, that man, he broke us all. You must not ask this of me."

"I ain't the one asking. Not really." There was a pause and then Fallon's voice continued. "We been called, Elizabeth. Look at me. Not gray. Silver. You too."

There was a gasp from Doctor Lisbet and then the crash of breaking glass. Cheyanne could stand it no longer and burst into the room.

At first it seemed like nothing had happened. Lisbet was standing next to a shelf where a bottle had fallen to the floor, one hand to her mouth, staring at Fallon. Cheyanne's gaze followed hers and she stared in disbelief, as well.

Because Fallon had taken off his smoked-lens spectacles. His eyes were revealed now, shining silver—not gray like Doctor Lisbet's, but unmistakably silver, with a glow of their own like blue-white fire.

Then Cheyanne realized that Lisbet's eyes had silvered as well.

"It's happening now," Fallon said, his voice rough. "Not in fifty years or ten or five. *Now.* Are you with me or not?"

• • •

For a moment there was silence in the little cabin. Finally Fallon shook his head and put his dark spectacles back on, concealing the eerie silver irises of his eyes. "It's past sundown now," he said. "I ain't had a real meal or slept in a bed in the last nine days. They tell me the Jarvis lady puts on a nice spread and she has rooms to let. That's where I'll be. I expect to leave around noon tomorrow."

"Where?" Lisbet swallowed and added, more firmly, "Do you even have a plan?"

Fallon snorted a laugh, but there was no real humor in it. "Why d'you think I'm here? You all are the plan. I heard Brainerd's up north, somewhere around Three Sisters. I'll try him next. Aaron's somewhere up that way too, I'll have to someways get a line on him. Hoping one of 'em might have heard something about Larry." He put his hat back on. "You think on what I said, Lisbet. I hope to see you in the morning." He tipped his hat at Cheyanne. "Miss Cheyanne."

The second the door closed after him, Cheyanne burst out, "What was all that? Who is he? Who's Anne-Marie? Are you…?"

Doctor Lisbet held up a hand. "Please, Cheyanne. I know you have a thousand questions. But … not yet. Please leave me be for a little while. Go out in the other room and put the kettle on. I think maybe some tea would help. I need… I need to think." Cheyanne saw that now that Fallon had gone, Lisbet's eyes no longer shone silver, but were back to their normal ash-gray. The doctor looked at her and managed a wan smile. "I will try and answer all your questions, dear one. But not just yet. Please, leave me."

It was not the usual no-nonsense tone she used when giving Cheyanne an errand, but rather, one that was almost pleading. *She looks like she might cry,* Cheyanne thought.

It was this last unprecedented, once-unthinkable realization more than anything else that kept her from bombarding Doctor Lisbet with more questions. Cheyanne went out to the pump and levered some water into the large teakettle, then brought it back in and set it on the stove. She sat behind the desk and stared unseeing at the patient records ledger she had been working on. It already seemed like years ago when Lucas had come in. Cheyanne closed the old leatherbound volume and thought, trying to make sense of what she had seen and heard.

Elizabeth Shaw had shown many sides of herself to Cheyanne in their time together, but never, not until today, had she looked so nakedly vulnerable.

Cheyanne did not know what to make of that. She had come to think of her guardian as an unshakable force of nature. But this man Fallon had shaken her. Him and his silver eyes. No wonder he wore those smoked-lens spectacles even at night.

The kettle began to whistle. Cheyanne went to the shelf where Lisbet kept a tin of the herbal tea that she had chopped and dried the previous summer. She spooned out the amount she knew the doctor liked into a mug, dumped boiling water over it, and then knocked on the consulting room door. "D—do you want tea?"

She heard Lisbet sigh. "Yes, Cheyanne. Come on in and sit with me."

Cheyanne entered the room and wordlessly handed Lisbet the steaming mug. Lisbet sipped it, smiled, and then looked over the rim of the mug at Cheyanne. "My word but your eyes are wide. I am sorry, dear. I suppose all this must seem rather frightening."

It frightens you, Cheyanne thought but did not say. Instead she said softly, "Who is that man? Fallon?"

"He's… an old friend. I guess you could say we studied together. For a time we were like brother and sister. Us and the others, we were a family of sorts. But it all went very wrong. I thought I had left it behind me."

Cheyanne couldn't help it. She blurted, "Is that what you were hiding from? Why you came here?"

Doctor Lisbet quirked an eyebrow and considered it. "Hiding? Not consciously, not really. No one was hunting me. I thought everyone from those days was dead. No, I wanted… I just wanted to live my life and practice medicine. Live quietly. Without *drama*," she added, in an exasperated tone. "Even in death that woman foments drama. It was her gift and her curse."

"Who?" Cheyanne paused, then plunged ahead. "The name he said… Anne-Marie? Who was she?"

"I'm not sure I can answer that, little one. Not even to this day. And I knew her better than anyone, except possibly for Jonas." She shook her head. "She was the sister of my heart and the bane of us all, she was light and laughter and suicide and sin, and you never knew which you would get on a given day."

"I don't understand."

"I don't either." Doctor Lisbet let out a curt bark of bitter laughter. Like Fallon's a short while before, it was utterly without humor. "But I will try and tell you what I remember of those days. Maybe it will help both of us to come to some understanding."

Two
The Cliff & the Ravens (Lisbet's Story)

Elizabeth Shaw had come to the desert to die.

The diagnosis seven months ago had been harsh but indisputable. Her colleague at the Boston hospital knew better than to sugar-coat it for her or attempt to obfuscate the matter with a lot of jargon, and such would have been wasted on her anyway. She had run the tests herself twice before even seeking out a second opinion. Elizabeth did not like to delegate her lab work. The science was too new, even in a town like Boston. Anyway she did not think much of the man who ran the laboratory department at Massachusetts General (she had been planning to bring his shortcomings to the attention of the Board of Governors at the next meeting, until her own medical crisis demanded her full attention.) So she had sought out another doctor friend whom she respected and simply given him the samples and told him to run the tests, and the answer was exactly as grim as she expected.

Leukämie, they called it. A cancer of the blood, a disease hardly anyone knew of as yet. The German doctor whose name she couldn't remember had only published his findings a couple of decades previously, in 1847, and it was damnably difficult on this side of the Atlantic to get hard data from any but the most urban hospitals. New York, Boston, Philadelphia, maybe Chicago—that was it. Even at those places no one was studying this disease and west of there, medicine in America was largely at the level of poultices and leeches. No, London was where the research was being done and she thought briefly about buying passage there and burning through her savings in an effort to race the calendar seeking a treatment, if she could secure a post at one of the big hospitals. Or possibly Paris. She had four languages and was reasonably fluent, but she quailed at the thought of trying to do state-of-the-art biological research in a foreign tongue.

In her heart she knew it was futile. She was brilliant but not genius-breakthrough-brilliant, and after doing more research she had realized that even a palliative treatment for this disorder would take a genius-level breakthrough. She had sought out the journals in the original German and pored over them, but there was no hope of a cure as yet. No one was even sure where the sudden, inexplicably deformed white-cell growth originated, though there had been some theories about the marrow of the bones being the source.

By then Elizabeth's interest was lagging, as she realized there was no science to help her. A kind of bleak, bitter acceptance took the place of her desperate efforts at research. Of course she was going to die of something no one had ever heard of, nothing her family would comprehend. They would doubtless ascribe it to some moral failing on her part. She had defied their expectations time and again, ever since she had eschewed settling down with some young society buck from the pack in Baltimore in favor of college and a degree in medicine. She had hardly paid any attention to her parents' horror then and she certainly had not for a moment thought about confiding in them when she had been diagnosed. Once she had confirmed to her satisfaction that there was nothing to be done, her practical nature had reasserted itself. *I have a year; what shall I do with it?*

Travel, came the answer. To the great Western frontier. She hungered to see new places, to see a different kind of country. To go beyond the horizon.

Desert country. Further research showed (Elizabeth Shaw was a great believer in thorough research as a prelude to action) that she could travel by rail as far as Great Salt Lake, and then by stage to the gold diggings at Canyon City. After that it would have to be on horseback or on foot; there were no wagon trails to speak of in the direction she intended to take. She was not interested in the roaring boisterousness of gold-fever towns like Canyon City or Whiskey Gulch. She intended to go west from Canyon City towards Warm Springs. She did not admit, even to herself, of the possibility that perhaps the shamans of the native aboriginal population might have in their superstitious ignorance stumbled upon a new kind of drug therapy in their ritual smoking of herbs and ingesting of roots, but she *had* heard anecdotal accounts of miracle cancer cures achieved by the medicine men of the Umatilla and Paiute tribes somewhere in the central Oregon territory. The possibility was lurking there, just beneath conscious thought.

And what else did she have to do with her time, anyway? Why not go and visit the wild Indians and see the legendary Painted Hills? Cure or no, it was long past time for her to get away from all the tiresome gossip and gamesmanship that went along with doctor's residency in a big city hospital. To say nothing of the constant necessity of proving her skills to fools who had none, simply because of her gender. She had devoted her adult life to being of service to others. It was damned well time for her to serve herself, now that time was short.

Once Elizabeth made up her mind on a course of action, she was an unstoppable force. She quietly closed down her practice, tendered her resignation at Mass General and also from the various professional societies she had bullied her way into a few years before, and set about provisioning herself for a journey west. She traded her fine silk dresses and Parisian hats in for a long leather duster (the fringe, she thought, made for a rather dashing and adventuresome look), practical cotton shirts and denim riding trousers, and soft suede boots. She also, after a long discussion with a male friend who had just returned from Wyoming, decided it would be prudent to arm herself, and invested in a .32 rimfire

"Travel…to the great Western frontier."

Smith and Wesson revolver, one of the new Rollin White models. Her friend was kind enough to spend a couple of afternoons demonstrating its use to her, and when those lessons were concluded she was satisfied that she was competent to defend herself from wolves or cougars—or men.

The early part of her journey had gone well enough. The rail and stagecoach journeys had been made without incident. She had spent an extra week in Dayville seeing to a miner's compound fracture, simply because she happened to be disembarking from her stagecoach across the street from where the unfortunate man's horse threw him, but the bag of gold dust he offered in payment was more than enough to provision her for the journey westward. Once she was satisfied the miner's fracture was not going to turn septic (she had been forced to treat the wound with gin purchased from the saloon, since there was no real hospital anywhere within five hundred miles, and no carbolic to be had) she returned her attention to her explorations. She invested most of the grateful miner's payment in a mule that she dubbed Pytheas, after the ancient Greek explorer. This was soon shortened to Pye. The rest of her funds she spent on filling her saddlebags with dried meats and vegetables, and cartridges for the .32.

Then, with no ceremony at all, she had set out on almost a direct line west, depending on the distant Bachelor Butte to keep herself oriented. Most of the maps she had studied referred to this area simply as "Sage Desert," with few to no landmarks noted between her and the Cascade mountains. A couple of them had simply scrawled, *Injun country*. That suited Elizabeth just fine.

To her mild surprise, her disease had shown few symptoms as yet. She tired a little more easily than she used to, and bruises seemed to happen more frequently and took longer to heal. Some days she ached so badly it was all she could do to make ten miles. But overall, she still felt relatively healthy.

The desert climate suited her, she found. This was also something of a surprise. Back east, she had loathed summer, with the heat and the sweaty crowds and the stinking effluence of overworked horses in the streets and rotting kitchen refuse littering the alleys. But it was late autumn now, and though the nights were bitterly cold, the days were dry and pleasantly warm. She fell into a routine of walking in the mornings, stopping for some sort of lunch as the sun grew high, then napping for a couple of hours until it cooled enough to travel a few more miles, stopping to make camp as the sun set. Sometimes she rode Pye, but it seemed an unfair burden to her and she never could bring herself to do it for any length of time, though the mule never balked or protested. More often she just walked with him, content to let him carry the supplies. She had found a river that flowed west more or less in the direction she was going, and they followed it... but it banked north on her fifth day out from Canyon City.

Faced with the decision to continue west or follow the river north, she had decided to follow the river, on the theory that she needed the water and therefore any Indian tribes in the area also would be near the water. But after the second day she discovered that the cliffs on either side of the river were rising in spectacularly beautiful – but practically impassable – sheer red walls of crumbling rock and shale. *Well, they called it Canyon City for a reason,* she thought ruefully, and kept going.

On the fifth day, though, the meager shoreline at the foot of the western cliff wall that she and Pye had been traveling along disappeared, leaving only rushing rapids that disappeared between impossibly high cliffs on either side.

Elizabeth sighed and said a word that nice ladies did not normally use. Then she halted and leaned on a boulder, considering her options. Pye looked at her with wide trusting eyes and for a moment she felt irrationally guilty at leading the faithful animal into such a place. There was not even any wild grass here for him to snack on.

Well, there was nothing for it but to backtrack; she would retrace her path along the strip of shore and try to find a trail up to the top of the cliffs. The alternative would have been to return all the way to the canyon entrance and start over, losing the last three days' travel; and she was too stubborn to accept that option without at least looking for a trail that would allow her to continue forward. There must be wildlife in the area that used the river to drink, she reasoned, therefore there must be some sort of path they used to reach the water. Q.E.D.

She and her blessedly even-tempered and obedient mule had only been picking their way back along the shore for an hour or so when she saw the ravens.

She counted five at first, but more continued to land, until there were— what? Nine? Ten? No, fourteen in all. They were roosting in a diagonal along the cliff face, almost in a line. *Like soldiers,* Elizabeth thought. *Or sentries.*

Once the thought struck her, she could not shake it, as absurd as it seemed. She stopped to look at them. What were they roosting on, anyway? Was that—it was! A path of sorts. "Spirit guides!" she blurted. "Why not?"

Pye cocked his head at her as if in skeptical response. She laughed at his expression and at her own absurdity. Nevertheless, though she did not truly believe in omens, they seemed to portend good fortune. She knew that ravens were regarded as harbingers, even sacred, by many of the western tribes.

Well, then! Where did that diagonal line of black birds end, anyway? Downward and to her left... She looked around the foot of the cliff and saw a narrow cut behind one boulder that was just barely wide enough for her and the mule. It seemed as though they *had* guided her. Excited now at finding a solution to her dilemma, she tugged on Pye's reins and they started up the path, hugging the cliff face.

It was slow going. Some of the time the trail was hardly more than a bit of shelf sticking out from the cliff side, and the ground itself was treacherous, strewn with pebbles and sand that made it easy to slip. She had to pick her steps carefully and at one point even stopped to re-position the saddlebags and bedroll so Pye would not be pushed too far towards the edge. But the path was wide enough to admit the mule as long as they did not move with undue haste. Fortunately, she did not suffer from vertigo, or the sheer drop to her right would have dizzied and paralyzed her. Pye followed with the same trusting obedience he had shown ever since she acquired him; she held the reins in one hand, leading him the way a society matron might walk her poodle.

Until they reached a certain point, roughly two-thirds of the way up. Suddenly the mule froze, refusing to advance any further. Elizabeth urged him, tugged a little harder, then really pulled. The animal jerked his head back and brayed a protest.

Elizabeth swore again, this time with real savagery. Of all the times for her normally sweet-natured mule to demonstrate the stubbornness for which his species was famed. What was she to do? She couldn't very well drag him. The path was too narrow for her to get behind the animal to chivvy him forward, and even if she could get back there to try it, if he should kick in protest, there would be no dodging it; that would be the end of her. "Damn it, Pye. What is the *problem*? The path is not even as narrow here as it was below. Come on." She yanked on the reins, hard.

And her foot slipped. She spun, fell, and the path crumbled beneath her. Suddenly she was dangling over the cliff, a spray of dirt and rocks cascading around her. She clung to the reins that were now her only lifeline. Pye brayed in hurt and fear and shook his head, trying to back away, and then the path beneath him crumbled as well. Almost in slow motion, mule and woman both slid in a tumble of shale and pebbles out into open space. *He was trying to warn me,* Elizabeth thought in horror as she fell. *And I didn't listen—*

Then her head cracked against a granite outcropping, and she knew no more.

• • •

Elizabeth was awakened by the agonized lowing coming from the mule. She opened her eyes and saw that the two of them lay in an impossible tangle, half-buried in dry, crumbling red clay and bits of shale. They were perhaps halfway down the cliff face, lying on the outcropping that had broken their fall and kept them from a fatal plunge all the way to the bottom. Elizabeth saw that both of the mule's forelegs were bloody and broken, with a bone splinter showing on the left. Pye lay between her and the sheer drop on her right, partially hanging over the edge. *Faithful helper to the end,* she thought. *His body blocked my fall… saved my life.*

She did the only thing she could for him—reached into her vest for the .32 and shot him in the head. It took two bullets to put him down. The impact was enough to shift his weight and the dead animal slid off the outcropping, falling hundreds of feet to the river below. Bile rose in Elizabeth's throat as she heard the meaty smack of the mule's body hitting the rocks at the bottom.

Poor thing. My fault. Serves him right for trusting me. My arrogance has condemned us both. Her eyes bright with tears, Elizabeth struggled to sit up—and screamed as blinding, searing pain shot up her leg clear into her torso. Her leg was broken too, she realized. She couldn't move. And all her supplies, food, water, everything, had just fallen to the bottom of the canyon with her dead mule.

But I still have the pistol, she thought. Four cartridges left in the cylinder. She could end it right now.

Elizabeth considered it. She was a doctor and knew the reality of her situation. There was no conceivable way out for her, trapped on the cliff side as she was. Even if she had been uninjured, she was hundreds of feet up and had no rope. There was no visible path from her position, or even footholds to climb, and it would have taken the skill of a circus acrobat to leave the tiny outcropping where she lay.

But it was a moot point. She dared not move without first immobilizing the broken bones in her leg. And that was impossible as well, even if she had something to kill the pain. (Which she did not; her few medical supplies were in the saddlebags along with her other provisions.) There was nothing here in this pile of dirt with which to improvise a splint. Any attempt to move without one, given the splintered bone in her leg, would likely sever a major blood vessel, possibly even puncture the femoral artery. Certainly the kind of movement required to climb up or down from where she was would tear the muscle in such a way as to leave her far worse off. Likely damage the nerves as well, possibly to the point where she would never walk again. As it was, she was certain she would limp for the rest of her days even if she were to be rescued somehow.

The rest of her days were few in any case. Her gaze turned to the pistol in her hand. She could think of no reason not to use it. Why not just end it?

She might have shot herself at that moment but for the distraction of the ravens, again. Two of the birds landed at her feet and regarded her with beady black eyes.

"Well?" she croaked. "What do you want now? As guides you are clearly worthless," she added, and spat. It was pink.

Internal bleeding as well, then. She probably would measure the rest of her life in hours. Better to go cleanly, with a clear head, although she felt vaguely angry about ending her journey so ignobly. A meal for these damned carrion crows. Well, so be it. Grimly, she turned the pistol in her hand and looked thoughtfully down the barrel. In the mouth would be best. Through the soft tissue at the top.

Then the miracle happened.

"Hello? Is someone down there?" A girl's voice. "Ezekiel! The ravens were right…there's been a rockfall! I think there's a woman trapped on the cliff!"

Elizabeth struggled to sit up. "I'm here!" she screamed. Or she thought she did. What came out was more like an animal cry, *Mheeerrrrgh,* and then a spasm of coughing. She dribbled a bright red gout of blood down the front of her shirt and passed out.

● ● ●

She awoke lying on a cot in a tidy but sparely-furnished shack. Sunlight streamed through the room's one window, lighting everything with a golden glow. Someone had removed her torn and bloodied clothing, and she was now clad in a simple flannel night-dress. She was propped up in a partially sitting position on a pile of coarse pillows, covered with a quilt that had a bright flower pattern sewn into its patches.

Elizabeth sat up, blinking, trying to make sense of it all. This effort exhausted her and she fell back.

"Oh, you're awake! I'm so glad. But you mustn't move. You have the singing in your blood yet. You must let it run its course."

It was a blonde girl, surely no more than nineteen years of age. She wore a simple gingham dress, checked white and yellow. In the sunlight, with her blonde hair, she looked as though she were glowing. She continued, "We weren't sure the healing would take. You were in terrible shape when we found you, and Ezekiel divined that you had a disease of the blood as well. It was that which made it so complex. But you should be well soon."

"My leg—" Abruptly Elizabeth realized that she felt no pain. But not as though she had been drugged or benumbed. No, she felt… *well*. Healed. It dawned on her that in fact she felt better than she had at any time in the last year. She moved her leg, experimentally, and it responded with no discomfort at all.

The bones had completely knitted. She could move her legs freely. She drew her knees up and then straightened both legs. No pain. No muscle or nerve damage. No loss of function at all.

"H-how long have I been asleep?" she whispered, horrified. For the leg to have healed so thoroughly—she must have been in a coma. For months. Years, possibly? Dear God.

But then I would be dead. The blood cancer… None of this made any sense. "How long?" she asked, again, with urgency.

"Oh, just about the clock around, I imagine. From yesterday afternoon when we found you until just now, it's barely another couple of hours before sunset, I think—we don't really use clocks here," she added, apologetically. "We had to keep you unconscious longer than we normally would when we used the soulsong. Because of the blood disease, you see. The bones were simple, but the blood was a struggle. Any of us could have managed your leg and the ribs, but it took Ezekiel to purify your blood of the… I can't pronounce it. Ezekiel said it was German."

"*Leukämie,*" Elizabeth said, automatically. Her mind was still trying to process the words she had just heard. What the girl was telling her… it was medically impossible. She must have misunderstood her. "Are you saying… you found me yesterday? My leg was not broken after all?"

The blonde girl laughed. "Oh no, your leg was *shattered*. And you had three broken ribs, too. One tore your lung. If the ravens hadn't told us where you were you would have been dead by sundown. Anyway, bones are easy. All of us have learned how to heal those. You'll see. If you stay, that is," she added. "Please, I do so hope you will. It gets tiresome being the only girl. But I'm so foolish prattling on like this, you must be exhausted. You just rest now. I'll stop."

"But—" Elizabeth shook her head. "This—it's impossible. Who are you? What is this place? How...?"

"I'm Anne-Marie, and this is Stonegarden Abbey. The rest... well, we had best wait for Ezekiel. He will explain it all for you. I promise. Rest now."

Elizabeth could think of no reason to argue, and sank back into the pillows. She was asleep again in moments.

• • •

She awoke again just as the sun was setting. This time she let herself just lie still, trying to get a sense of her condition. She still felt... could it even be possible? That she was whole again? Healed of not just her broken bones, but of the cancerous blood disease as well?

"You are indeed well again. It is not a dream."

There was a man standing at the foot of her cot, smiling. He was older, balding, but with a salt-and-pepper fringe of hair coming around his ears into a full beard. He was dressed in denim overalls over a plain white shirt, and might have been a farmer but for the odd amulet he wore on a gold chain around his neck. It was an asymmetrical oval, and appeared to have been fashioned out of onyx, or perhaps obsidian, veined with gold. The bearded man regarded her with pale blue eyes that seemed to twinkle with some secret amusement.

Elizabeth sat up and flexed her arms a little. She returned his look with a direct and quizzical eye. "I cannot dispute it," she admitted. "Impossible as it seems. The evidence is inarguable. But... I am baffled as to how. No medicine I am aware of can mend bone like that in less than a day. It really has been just a day?"

"Almost two, now," admitted the older man. "Your case was probably the most ambitious undertaking we have attempted in our time here; I confess that I was so exhausted afterward that I slept a great deal of the day away myself. But I am forgetting the niceties. Allow me to welcome you to our little enclave here at Stonegarden. I am Ezekiel Reardon. And you? We know much of you but not your name, nor what brought you to us."

"I am Elizabeth Shaw." She paused, then added, "A medical doctor from Boston, but I left that behind me some months ago."

"Because of the cancer?" Ezekiel raised an eyebrow. "It is gone now, you know."

"I do not know any such thing," Elizabeth snapped. "I am grateful for the help, truly, but I am tired of these oblique and impenetrable references. Please, let us have plain words. What is this place? The girl—Anne-Marie— she called this an abbey? Is this some sort of monastery? Who are you? What did you do to me?"

Ezekiel chuckled and held up a hand. "I apologize. We are unduly cautious, probably. We are circumspect with newcomers, because we have grown to expect a degree of superstition and hostility from those that come across our group. Anne-Marie likes to call this an abbey because of our isolation and our devotion to intellect. It is her little joke."

"You are not a church, then?"

"Not in the traditional sense, no, though there is a spiritual component to our studies." Ezekiel smiled and shrugged. "Titles are meaningless. We are not a church or a college but we are immersed in the sort of work that could be found at either. In truth we are very few. Just a small gathering of scholars, trying to broaden the knowledge of man."

"This knowledge you refer to. That is what healed me? Because if it is …I don't even have words." Elizabeth shook her head and then leaned forward. "Speeding the healing of shattered bones is miraculous in itself. But if you have in fact freed me of the *leukämie* poisoning my blood as well, you have made a discovery on a level with the germ theory of infection. I have studied medical and biological science for most of my adult life and there is nothing anywhere remotely resembling the cure you have provided me. It will revolutionize the face of medicine."

"Revolution. Yes, that is what we would face." The bearded man's voice was thoughtful. "Such knowledge comes with a cost. Man is often reluctant to embrace a truth that threatens his beliefs."

"I am not threatened by facts, ever," Elizabeth said firmly. "I am a scientist. Do not think me some fragile flower of womanhood given to swooning at unpleasant news. I have seen more than my share of blood and ugliness just working in a large hospital, to say nothing of what transpires here on the frontier. A discovery as profound as this… It must be shared. Think of the lives that could be saved, as you apparently saved mine."

Ezekiel nodded. "Well said." He smiled a little. "Would you be willing to back those words with action, then? Join us here in our work?"

"What work?"

Ezekiel considered it. "Your clothing and belongings, what we could salvage from the pack animal we found dead at the foot of the canyon, are in the cabinet here." He moved to the door. "Put on some fresh clothes and join me outside, and I will show you."

• • •

Elizabeth soon was dressed in her usual denim trousers and cotton shirt, and donned her long duster as well. She noted with pleasure that the .32 had been cleaned and placed in the cabinet along with the other contents of her saddlebags. She thought about putting the gun in the pocket of her coat and then decided that was absurd. There was no threat to her here. And she was burning with curiosity now, especially since arising and dressing. The more she moved, the more she realized how easily the motion came to her limbs now. The dull aches in her joints, that she had grown accustomed to simply enduring, were completely gone. She was more than healed. She felt years younger. She felt like running, singing, dancing, twirling about like a giddy schoolgirl. Instead, she composed herself and stepped outside the little shack.

Ezekiel was waiting, with a couple of others. "Anne-Marie you met earlier. This is Jonas, and over here are Lawrence and Theo. There are others, but they are engaged in their work at the moment. Everyone, this is Elizabeth Shaw, a medical doctor and clearly a woman of remarkable erudition." He paused. "Dr. Shaw is considering joining us. Please make her welcome."

Anne-Marie darted forward and gave her a quick embrace. "Don't be so formal, Ezekiel," she said over her shoulder. "You'll frighten her off. Anyone would think you were initiating her into the Freemasons or something." She turned to Elizabeth. "Can I call you Elizabeth?"

"Lisbet is what my friends usually use," Elizabeth felt ridiculously awkward. "Please call me that. All of you," she added. "I think my doctoring days may well be done, given your skills here. I doubt I can keep up."

"You'll do, I think." This was Jonas. He was tall, dark-haired, with deep brown eyes that held wry humor. "Smart woman outpaces most men, most times. Woman smart enough to be a doctor means you'll be leaving us all in the dust soon enough."

"How evolved of you, Jonas." Lawrence rolled his eyes. He was whippet-thin, with close-cropped black hair and pale green eyes that gave him a sort of feline look. "And here we all thought you were just here to tend the horses and do the heavy lifting."

Jonas took no offense but merely grinned. "Somebody has to tote the meat up to the lodge. It's honest work. Leastways nobody ever tried hanging *me*, Larry."

"Lawrence." The slender man glared at Jonas.

"He prefers Lawrence but go ahead and just call him Larry, he puts on airs if you don't," Anne-Marie told Elizabeth in an exaggerated *sotto voce,* then giggled. Lawrence sighed and shook his head in mock exasperation, which only made Anne-Marie giggle even more. It broke the tension and everyone laughed, even Elizabeth. It was impossible not to.

Somehow, in that moment of laughter, she felt a wave of sudden friendship for these people. She had never really had friends before, only colleagues. But here… Perhaps her miraculous physical rejuvenation was the first step to a new way of living for her, one without anger and competition, just the joy of learning. Not in all her life had Elizabeth ever been faced with such easy acceptance, without having to constantly prove herself or demand respect for her education and intelligence. It seemed that the group wanted her with them because of her intellect, not in spite of it. She had not dared to dream such a place existed, but here she was. How could she turn her back on that? She was curious about what Ezekiel wanted to show her, certainly, but she had already made up her mind to join them in their work, whatever it was.

Ezekiel waved a hand. "Run along now, the lot of you. I just wanted you to meet …Lisbet, is it?" Elizabeth nodded. "Anyway. I wanted to introduce you to her before we go and look at the diggings. Lisbet, if you will follow me? I trust you are up to a walk."

"Honestly? I feel I could bound along the trail like a wild deer," Elizabeth said. "I am not sure how long this euphoric sense of well-being will last, but—"

"The rest of your life, if you choose." Ezekiel grinned. "Come, I'll show you what we have found."

The others nodded and went in different directions, leaving Elizabeth and Ezekiel alone. She took the moment to look around her and try to assess her surroundings. The abbey had been constructed on a bluff overlooking the canyon. Beyond, further up, she could see a few bits of vegetation and some brown and withered scrub trees along the ridge, but the landscape was mostly bare rock, the crumbling red shale that had so nearly been her doom. The only truly stable part of their surroundings was where they stood now, a small clearing that was largely a flat granite plateau covered with a spraying of sand. Ezekiel led her past a row of small cabins similar to the one in which she had awoken, to a somewhat larger building that stood overlooking the others. It looked a bit like a church and she asked Ezekiel if that was in fact what it was.

He laughed. "Anne-Marie and Jonas and Aaron would say yes, Lawrence and Theo and Philip would say no. Myself, I would say it was both, and neither."

"I thought we had agreed to speak plainly." Elizabeth smiled to take some of the bite out of it. "What would you call it, then?"

Ezekiel did not answer right away. Instead of entering the small wooden building as she thought he intended they should, he stopped and leaned on the whitewashed planking of the wall. It was almost full dark now. Finally he said, "Do you know of Hermes Trismegistus? The Hermetic arts?"

The allusion was maddeningly familiar to Elizabeth, but the memory lay just out of reach. Something in college, before medicine had become her course of study. Something from history… then she had it. "He was… an alchemist, I think, yes? Long ago."

"More of a philosopher and theorist." Ezekiel looked pleased. "But it's nice you knew even that much. Trismegistus, 'thrice-great,' was the name given to him for his mastery of astrology, alchemy, and theurgy. The governing principles of all creation."

"Theurgy? Like theology?"

"Theology is the study of religion. Therugy is the mastery of it. The practices to summon and join with the divine."

Elizabeth stared at Ezekiel in disbelief. "But you said this was not truly a church. These things, alchemy and whatnot, are all long discredited. I thought you said what you discovered was science."

Ezekiel held up a finger, admonishing her. "No. You assumed that. We have moved beyond science here, though there is a scientific principle underlying it. Let me ask you this—have you studied a foreign language, ever?"

Elizabeth blinked. What was he getting at? "I have four languages. English, French, Italian, and German. A smattering of Spanish. What you are saying makes no sense in any of them," she added, tartly.

She had meant the remark to deflate him and prod him forward, but this delighted him. "Yes! Exactly! This is the key point. Are you aware that language shapes thought?"

"Well, of course it does—"

"No." Ezekiel made a noise of impatience. "I do not mean matters of philosophy or literature. I speak of brain function itself, doctor. For example, a human child, should it be allowed to reach a certain age without learning to speak, will forever be cursed with mental retardation. We need language not just to communicate but to *think*, to allow our minds to work at all. Consciousness itself can be categorized as an internal conversation we have for our entire lives. You surely knew this?"

"I knew of the necessity of language for healthy infant development, certainly," Elizabeth was struggling to keep up. "But I cannot see the relevance of that fact to the medical miracle you apparently performed upon me."

"I'm getting there." Ezekiel was enjoying her consternation, something Elizabeth was beginning to find hugely irritating. He opened the door to the not-quite-a-church they stood in front of and gestured for her to enter. She did so, with Ezekiel following close behind.

She saw that there was no floor but simple bare rock. In fact the building itself, she realized, was little more than a façade. It was taller than the others because it had been constructed to cover a series of roughly-hewn stone pillars standing in a semicircle surrounding what looked at first to be black gravel, but which she saw upon closer examination was actually a pile of obsidian chips, black glass veined with gold, like the one Ezekiel's amulet had been made from. She abruptly realized that there was light in the room, but not from any lamp or candle. Somehow it was coming from the pool of shattered black glass in the center of the obelisks, but despite this golden glow, the rocks themselves remained black and largely opaque.

"What is this?" she whispered.

"After some fourteen years of study, I have concluded that this is all that remains of a temple constructed by a previously unknown aboriginal tribe," Ezekiel's voice came from behind her. "They called themselves the Kuyagah. They used the Language that Hermes Trismegistus only speculated might exist. The Language that changes the shape of the human brain into a configuration that lets it perceive the underlying structure of the universe. And once you can see that, you can manipulate it." He said something further, something that was no language Elizabeth could recognize, in a tone both as musical to the ear as a gentle choir and as jangling to the nerves as breaking glass. There was a flare of light and suddenly the semi-circle of ugly stone pillars shone with golden letters— no, runes, carvings, something… she could not make sense of it, and it hurt her eyes to look at it; not with brightness, but with… *otherness*.

She turned to face Ezekiel and saw him sitting with his legs folded… sitting in mid-air, with nothing beneath him. He glowed with the same golden light as the carvings, floating before her as easily as a child's toy would in a bath.

"What is this?"

"The Language of magic," he said. "That is what we study here. You will join us?"

Elizabeth could not speak for a moment. She realized her eyes had filled with tears. She understood, now. "Of course I will. As long as it takes."

"It will likely take a lifetime."

"Then… my life is yours."

She did not realize how true that would be, nor the consequences. Had Elizabeth Shaw thought she was selling her soul, she might have paused… but in that moment, her being suffused with the golden glow that Ezekiel and his people had gifted her with, all she could think was that she could ask nothing more of her life than to live it inside this miracle.

● ● ●

"That was how it began," Doctor Lisbet told Cheyanne. "I stayed and learned what I could of the Kuyagah. Almost a year. I became somewhat proficient with Language, but never as gifted as Anne-Marie or Ezekiel. Then… something happened. Something bad." She shook her head. "To this day I am not sure what. There had been tension. Quarrels within the group. I know Anne-Marie was at the center of it all but I couldn't tell you what it was about, all my attention was on my studies. You know how I feel about other people's dramas." She sighed. "I never did hear what was at the root of it. All I truly know was one night Jonas was shaking me awake, telling me to take Sultan and get out, ride as far as I could, something was coming. The entire camp was in flames. He practically heaved me atop the animal and slapped its rump, and Sultan was already spooked. He ran and it was all I could do just to hang on. By the time I got control of him and reined him in, we were almost a mile further up the ridge. I was turning him around to look back at Stonegarden, trying to see what was happening, when suddenly there was a huge explosion from the camp and fire blazed into the sky, and the earth itself shook and cracked beneath us." She paused and Cheyanne saw that her eyes had welled up a little.

"Our little group of social misfits," Doctor Lisbet said at last. "As I got to know them, I saw that none of us had a place in the world until Ezekiel gave us one. More, he gave us each other. The students, the abbey… they were my family. And I abandoned them, to my eternal shame. I ran. I thought they must be dead. I was sure, as I saw that great burst of flame, that I felt Anne-Marie screaming something in the old tongue. That somehow it was her the flames wanted. I *felt* it. Almost like a shove. If it is possible to be shoved by a wave of pure emotion. And then… nothing. They were all gone, and I was alone again."

"But… if there was a big fire—" Cheyanne did not want Doctor Lisbet to cry. "There wasn't anything you could do."

Doctor Lisbet's mouth quirked in a rueful smile. "Bless you, child, that's not the point. Jonas turned back after I was away because he was focused on rescue, that was his role with all of us, especially Anne-Marie. But I didn't even try. I was only focused on saving my own life. But it appears …I have been called on to rescue Anne-Marie after all."

Cheyanne had a million questions and could hardly manage to get even one out, there were so many crowding her thoughts all at once. "The Language? That was what you did with the wolf that time," she blurted. "And other times—"

"I am much less proficient than I was," Doctor Lisbet said. "I found that when I use it, I can feel Anne-Marie's cry of terror and pain again, as raw as it was that terrible night ten years ago. It is… I cannot bear it, that's all." Abruptly a small sob escaped her. "She was screaming for me, screaming for all of us, and I ran." She lowered her head into her arms. "I ran."

Cheyanne awkwardly put a hand on Doctor Lisbet's shoulder. She had more questions but she didn't want to ask them any more. She could think of nothing to say, and so she didn't say anything.

"There is something else." The older woman raised her head and looked at Cheyanne. "I have a confession. I have been circumspect because… well, for many reasons, but chief among them is because ignorance has been a kind of protection for you. But there is something you must know. Your mother—"

Cheyanne waited, not daring to say anything that might make Doctor Lisbet think better of admitting what she was about to admit.

"Your mother was Kuyagah, I think," Lisbet said at last. "She did not have the Language but I could sense it. It was her ancestry. It is a matter of… let us say, aura. There are a few left scattered across Washington and Oregon. Probably less than fifty, and I suspect none have studied the Language. When she came here—you likely were too young to remember, but you came from the east, from the same direction as Stonegarden. I think she was running from something in the desert, trying to save you and her unborn child from… I don't know what. She died too quickly. But it means you have it in your blood as well."

Cheyanne tried to make sense of this. "You mean I could do… magic?"

"It's not magic." Doctor Lisbet was firm. "It's a different system of science.

But certain bloodlines are more easily… I don't know how to explain it in terms you would understand. Suffice it to say that should you ever attempt to learn the Language you would find it came more easily to you. I do not recommend doing so," she added sharply. "In fact as your guardian I forbid it. But it also means—there may be threats to you. If what Jonas says is true—" Her voice trailed off, thoughtful. "You must guard yourself if I am not here, that's all." Doctor Lisbet looked up at Cheyanne with a touch of her usual brusqueness. "I suppose I better make a list for you to refer to with the patients. While I'm gone, you will have to—"

Cheyanne shook her head. "No."

The older woman stared for a second, disbelieving. "What?"

"No," Cheyanne said again. Her voice shook a little with the gravity of what she was doing, defying her mentor like this, but she would not be swayed. "I'm coming with you."

Three
Angry Johnny Reb (Fallon's Story)

They found Jonas Fallon at Birdie Jarvis's cafe the following morning, mopping up the last of his eggs with a toasted biscuit. He was still wearing his dark spectacles. "Good morning, ladies," he said. "Join me? The widow puts on the hell of a spread."

Doctor Lisbet shook her head. "No, we are just here to tell you that we shall be accompanying you. Don't leave without us. We must go home and pack and provision ourselves. Shall we meet you here in an hour's time?"

"Both of you?" Fallon looked appraisingly at Cheyanne. Even though she could not see his eyes—or perhaps because of that—she felt uncomfortable under his gaze. She glanced over at Doctor Lisbet to see if her eyes would turn silver again, but they remained their usual ash gray.

"Unless you can talk her out of it. I have had no success. Perhaps the two of you might chat while I pack and fetch our horses. Maybe you can change her mind, Jonas." With that, Doctor Lisbet swept out of the dining room, leaving Cheyanne standing alone, feeling shy and awkward.

Fallon gestured at the chair opposite his. "Well, have a seat, Miss Cheyanne. If'n you really want to come along at least tell me why. If Lisbet's told you about Stonegarden I'd think you'd be wanting to run in the other direction as fast as you can. Seems like it's a business you wouldn't want to mix in."

Cheyanne ignored this. Instead, she said, "What's wrong with your eyes?"

Fallon ignored that, in turn. He went on, "You want coffee? No, you girls are tea drinkers, I remember now. Let's see if Mrs. Jarvis has some tea for you." He popped the last of the roll in his mouth and chewed.

"I don't want tea. I want answers." Cheyanne's chin jutted out defiantly.

Fallon snorted with laughter. "By God, if you aren't Lisbet's daughter by blood you sure have her ways. She does just like that." He grew serious. "You answer mine and then I'll answer yours."

"All right." Cheyanne was a scrupulously fair-minded girl and this seemed fair. "Doctor Lisbet needs me. She's older now and it's a hard journey from here to the desert. She's helped so many folks it seems like it's her turn now for someone to help her. Anyway I don't want to stay here all alone."

"It's more than that." Fallon was looking at her very carefully. "You're half-breed Kuyagah, ain't you?"

"Doctor Lisbet thought so." Cheyanne blinked. "How did you know?"

"Aura. Got the knack of seeing such, after a time." This was the second time auras had been mentioned and Cheyanne was getting very curious. But before she could pursue it, Fallon shook his head. "Not important. What's important is she's frightened for you, isn't she."

It was not a question, not really. Cheyanne nodded.

"Don't you think she might know what she's talking about?"

"She won't *say*," Cheyanne burst out. "I don't understand what is so scary! If that place was all burned and everyone's dead... what's the harm? I just want to know what I came from. Who my father was. I don't see—"

"She's scared of the obsidian." Fallon cut her off. "I am too, tell the truth. We all been running, all of us who were there then and learned the Language. It changes you, not for the better. I know why Lisbet came here, it's because you can't feel that hellish rock through the earth here on the mountain the way you can in the desert country. But that makes no difference." He paused, trying to gather his thoughts.

Finally he went on, slowly. "I think...Lisbet 'n me 'n the others, we gotta do this thing, we have to go back. If'n our friend Anne is still alive—I can feel her, you know. The silver comes when I can hear her inside my head. Used to just be dreams but it's happening most all the while now, like a ringing in m'ears." He shrugged. "Getting stronger every day. It's why I started wearin' these." He tapped the spectacles. "The silvering, it was spookin' folks. But me… I can *feel* it. Like she's barely hangin' on, like this is the last chance. I know how it sounds, but I'll warrant Lisbet feels it too, whether she wants to own up to it or not. Feels her screaming for us. Pretty soon Lisbet's eyes will color same as mine all the time, not just every so often. It's her calling for our help. Only way to make it stop is to answer."

"Her. You mean Anne-Marie?"

Fallon nodded.

"What is the obsidian? Why does it want Anne-Marie?"

"I don't know that there's a name for it you would understand." Fallon's voice grew distant, remembering. "Not sure we ever understood, not really. We was kids playing with matches next to a jug of kerosene. And one night… it all went up in a big old explosion. Zeke Reardon knew it was coming, I'm sure. That crafty old bastard wanted it to happen. Why he did… well, we might never know that part of it." Fallon's brows knitted in an old anger. "It's on us, though, not him. We were fools to believe in him and ten years later we're still payin' for it." He straightened and looked directly at Cheyanne. "Lisbet wanted me to talk you out of it, but I think she's worried because you're part of this too. Somehow. Naught but two dozen Kuyagah left in the territory, if that, and one dropped on her doorstep? I don't believe in coincidence like that."

Cheyanne's eyes widened. "You think—my father might be someone from Stonegarden?" She took a deep breath, then plunged ahead. "Could Ezekiel be my father? Is he who my mother was running from?"

Fallon shook his head. "Ain't likely. We left him under two tons of rock, long before you ever met Lisbet." He paused. "You still hell-bent on this? Coming along?"

Cheyanne swallowed and nodded.

"Well. Then I guess I better tell you what you'll be getting into. The parts I know, anyways."

● ● ●

Jonas Fallon had fled into the desert to escape.

Escape what? He couldn't have given it a name. He had been running since before the end of the war, but from what, exactly… he wasn't sure. He had joined the Confederate Army largely because of his hatred for his father, the worst kind of Northern citified snob; talking about all sorts of highfalutin caring for mankind while using his money to screw the poor people of Chicago into the ground. Jonas wanted no part of his father's empire and ran away as soon as he could.

Siding with the Confederacy was just another way of rejecting all his family's hypocrisy and their plans for his life. But he soon discovered that he was a poor soldier, and that there was just as much hypocrisy in the Rebel ranks as there was back home. He learned quickly that gunfire and bloodshed were not heroic things at all; and more, he learned that he was surrounded by a bunch of other pointlessly angry young men who thought they were doing something noble, but at its core was built on an idea that was sick and rotting.

He had deserted his unit after they had shot a family of black folks who were just trying to get safely out of Virginia. Harmless civilians. Womenfolk, even, one with a baby. His sergeant had ordered them all executed as traitors, and no one had dared to raise an objection, not even Jonas himself. He realized then that he was as sickened by the war as he was by his family, and that he had merely exchanged one miserable situation for another. The cheers of the other soldiers filled him with self-loathing at being one of their number.

That night Jonas had shucked his uniform jacket and stolen the sergeant's horse, by far the best one in the unit, and lit out. He figured west was his best bet, somewhere away from the war. For the next couple of years he wandered with no clear goal other than to keep moving. He'd knocked around some in Colorado, done a brief stint mining copper in Utah, then found himself riding drag on a cattle herd in Montana.

No job held him for long. He couldn't ever seem to put any money together, and when he did most of it went to saloonkeepers. Drinking was the only thing that made him feel calm. Left to himself there was always the anger, seething just below the surface, with no real target except that of convenience. Though he could not have articulated this, somehow he was bitterly disappointed in himself but had no idea why. The frustration made him angry and the anger always sabotaged him in the end.

Eventually he had drifted into the enclave at Stonegarden and there, at last, he had found a kind of peace. Learning the Hermetic Language had filled the void in himself that drinking could not, given him the sense of ease and well-being that formerly he only could find in himself after three shots of rye. And there was no hangover.

For the first time in his adult life he found friends, as well. He enjoyed the company of all of his fellow scholars, even the lavender boys Larry and Theo. Somehow things didn't matter here the way they did in the world outside. Why, even that Nigra Aaron was just another one of them, and Fallon never gave any thought to the color of his skin any more than Aaron ever bothered about the fact that Jonas had served in the Reb army. They were all just Ezekiel's students, learning how to master the Language and the eerie golden power that came with it.

"This place is the first time I ever felt comfortable in m'own skin," he confided to Lisbet after her sixth month at Stonegarden. The two of them had formed a habit of walking in the mornings, just to look at the surrounding country along the ridge and enjoy the clean desert air before the heat became unbearable. Sometimes Anne-Marie came along as well, but more often they were alone. "Never would have thought it. Always figured a man like me would end up… I dunno. But studyin' old Injun rocks wasn't ever on the list, that's for damn sure."

"Nor myself," Lisbet laughed. "I assure you that I never pictured myself out here poring over ancient carvings when I was on staff at Massachusetts General. Though I daresay this choice would be as disappointing to my parents as was my decision to seek a medical degree."

"I imagine we're all disappointments to family in some measure." Fallon shrugged and smiled. "Maybe that's what calls us here. Seems like no one ever shows up here who ain't tarnished somehow."

"Really? Do tell. I am still getting to know the others." Lisbet smiled and gave Fallon a conspiratorial wink. "Do you have all the secrets then?"

"You'll never get Ezekiel to tell you how he got here, and Anne-Marie talks a lot without ever saying anything." Fallon snorted. "I can tell you that Larry and Theo are here because—well, it's obvious, ain't it? Them two got out of Idaho just barely ahead of a lynch mob, once word got out they was… well, you know." He fluttered a hand. "Aaron's here because it's about the only safe place for a Nigra here in Oregon, even though this weren't ever a slave state and the war's been over for a while now. They still hang black folks here if'n they think they plan on settling, or if they think a black boy's lookin' at a white gal the wrong way." He spat. "Every one of us here was running from something. Circumstances might be different but the result's the same. We're all here because we were looking for a way out of where we was at. I reckon Ezekiel and Anne-Marie were too. I just don't know the reason."

"So the work itself does not draw you?"

Fallon considered it. Finally he flashed Lisbet an embarrassed grin. "I don't know the true answer to that, Lisbet. I can feel the power in me same as you, all healthful and bouncy. I can't say I don't enjoy bein' able to use the Language. But I'm not *good* at it. Not like old Zeke or Anne-Marie, you look at them, they were practically born to it. The way they sang your blood clear, that was something to see."

"I'm sure it was." Lisbet smiled wryly. "Pity I slept through it."

But Fallon was still considering. "Larry's good, but it's not natural to him. You show real talent too. I don't think Theo cares much, and Aaron's happy just to be the camp cook, he ain't about learning the Language. He just likes it here. Philip, I don't know what his deal is, he don't talk much. I have a feeling he's more interested in Anne-Marie than anything, but she keeps him at a distance. Chances are that's gonna blow up into something one of these days that won't end well." He sighed. "But me... I try, but I'm never going to be more'n a jackleg magician compared to the rest of you. I'm here for the company, really."

"Well, I enjoy your company as well, Jonas." Lisbet smiled, then colored a little as she realized how that sounded. "That is—"

Fallon glanced at her. "You flirting with me, gorgeous?"

Lisbet's blush deepened. "Not at all! I... oh, damn you, Jonas Fallon, you..."

Fallon burst out laughing and waved it off. "I'm just funning with you, Dr. Shaw. Truth to tell, Ezekiel discourages that kind of thing. We're all just friends here. No need to get it all steamed up with a lot of man-woman drama."

"That is very wise." Lisbet nodded. Then her expression grew mischievous. "Was there a woman in your past at some point, then? You talk like a man who had something end badly."

Fallon snorted. "Most ever'thing I put my hand to ended badly till I got here, man-woman drama included. Looking back, it was m'own doing, though. I'm just glad I managed to light somewhere that'd take me. I don't even care about the work, not really. Happy to do the provisionin' and keep an eye out for Injuns and cougars and so on. You all can do the important learning and research and whatever. Me? I guess I'm here mostly 'cause I got tired of living alone."

"That's not so different than my own story," Lisbet admitted. "I too am pleasantly surprised at how comfortable all of you are to be around. Though I find the study of the Kuyagah stones themselves to be endlessly fascinating. To think what secrets we might unlock… wait, is that a rider?" She pointed further along the ridge, some hundred and fifty yards down, at a tiny silhouette visible on the path approaching Stonegarden.

"By God, it surely is," Fallon said. "Must've come along the top of the cliffs, above the place where you fell. Two of you in six months. Place is getting downright crowded. Guess we better go see what he's all about."

"Should we not fetch Ezekiel and the others?" Lisbet sounded nervous.

"Let's not panic. Might just be a feller passin' through." Fallon grinned. "We'll go say hello and be neighborly, see what he wants. Probably just food, not much that way he came but rocks and lizards. Come on, Lisbet."

Together they started down the hillside to where they could see the rider, now clearly visible as a man on a paint horse picking his way carefully up the ridge.

Then, from behind them, they heard the sound of hoofbeats. Fallon grabbed Lisbet's elbow and pulled her out of the way as Anne-Marie went thundering past them on her big black stallion, Sultan. Fallon swore. "Goddam it—that fool girl don't have any sense of—"

"No, look, Jonas." Lisbet pointed. "She has enhanced the horse with the Language. No normal animal could manage that ridge. His hooves are shining—"

"I see what she done to the horse. That's what I mean. Showing off to an outsider." Fallon's voice was grim. "Last thing we need." He started down the hillside to where Anne-Marie was already talking animatedly to the new arrival, without waiting for Lisbet to follow.

When he reached the two of them, Anne-Marie was bubbling with excitement. "Jonas! Look! The ravens said he was coming and here he is! Mr. Brainerd, this is Jonas Fallon, and coming up behind him there is Dr. Elizabeth Shaw."

The man on the paint horse looked drawn and tired, and his face was smeared with trail dust. He was very pale, and his hair, what they could see curling out from under the sweat-stained hat brim, was even lighter than Anne-Marie's, a blond that verged on white. By contrast, his eyes were very dark, a brown so deep it was almost black. Those dark eyes regarded the new arrivals with wary good humor as he nodded and tipped his hat. "Howdy. Nelson Brainerd, but folks call me Nels. You live up here in these cliffs?" He glanced ahead to the canyon walls rising on both sides of them, not quite believing it.

"We do," Fallon said, his voice curt. "Camp's a little further up."

"What in God's name you doing living up here in such a forsaken pile of rock?" Brainerd grinned, but the humor did not touch the dark eyes. They were full of cunning and suspicion.

Fallon kept it short, cutting Anne-Marie off as she was opening her mouth to answer. "Research. Archeology, you know, studying old Injun carvings and such."

Brainerd's mouth lifted in a sly smile. "Not mining?"

"There is some of that activity in these parts, yes, but the mining camps are closer to Canyon City," Lisbet put in brightly, ignoring the insinuation in Brainerd's words. "Back that way." She pointed. "If that's where you are headed I am certain Jonas can show you."

"But he's just got here!" This was Anne-Marie. "And the ravens spoke of him, he's meant for us!" Fallon glared at her and she burst out laughing. "Oh, don't be such a grump, Jonas. I know you think it's your job to mind me but I assure you Mr. Brainerd is no danger to us."

Brainerd smiled gratefully at this, but Fallon thought he saw something else there, too. The way he looked at Anne-Marie... damn it. Bad enough that Philip was getting cow-eyed over her, but a rivalry was even more worrisome. *Hellfire. That girl has a knack.* Fallon sighed. "Well, come on up the path with us and we can get you round some food. Water your horse. Ain't got much but it's better'n nothing."

"Yes, do. It's this way, but be careful of the path." Ignoring her own advice, Anne-Marie spun Sultan in almost a pirouette, so fast that it was nearly impossible to comprehend how she had turned the animal so easily on the narrow trail. Of course, it was in fact impossible without using magical aid. Fallon hoped the stranger wouldn't notice.

But he did. Brainerd stared after Anne-Marie as she and Sultan raced up the trail. "Ain't never seen a horse turn like that," he muttered. "Damn but that young lady can ride."

"Yes," Lisbet said, trying to divert him. "She and Sultan almost move as one sometimes, it is remarkable."

"Remarkable lady for sure." Confirming Fallon's worst suspicions, Brainerd's tone suggested he was no longer thinking about her horsemanship. He tapped his heels into the side of his own horse and they moved slowly up the trail after Anne-Marie.

Fallon snorted in disgust and turned to Lisbet. "Well, what's done is done. Guess we better go see what that fella's running from that brought him here."

"You think he's running?"

"We're all running, gorgeous. Thought we got that sorted out earlier." Fallon winked and flashed her a wry grin. "I'm just worried about who might be chasing this one." Without waiting for a response, he started up the trail back to Stonegarden, and Lisbet followed.

It took them about twenty minutes to get back to the little cluster of cabins. Though he could not help glancing back every so often, no one else appeared behind them. *Small blessings, anyway,* Fallon thought.

But as it turned out, Nelson Brainerd's arrival was not the only event to upset the routine at Stonegarden that day. When they arrived at the cabins, Ezekiel took Fallon aside. "Jonas, a moment, please." He led Fallon back out to an isolated place on the ridge just beyond the clearing where the cabins stood, overlooking the river far below. There he stopped and turned to face Fallon, his brow knitted with concern. "I wanted to let you know right away, Jonas, before you went looking. Philip is no longer with us."

Fallon blinked. "What?" This was not what he had been expecting.

"Philip left. Sometime in the night. We had words yesterday afternoon and apparently he took them to mean that I thought he should leave."

"But—" Fallon's eyes narrowed. "On foot? He won't get ten miles in this country without a horse."

"Of course he will." Ezekiel's tone held a slight edge of impatience. "You are still thinking like an outsider. With the Language, even a smattering, Philip can go anywhere he wishes with impunity. And he wishes… to be here no longer." He shrugged. "It's done. I just wanted to save you concerning yourself over it before you mounted some sort of search."

"You're not worried?"

"No reason to be. Philip will not speak of us to anyone."

"What was the quarrel about?"

Ezekiel waved a hand. "Not important. He was a very emotional fellow. Bruised easily. Probably for the best that he's gone." There was a brief bray of laughter from back at the cluster of cabins. Ezekiel turned and eyed the rest of the group, where Anne-Marie was introducing Brainerd to the others. "What do you think of our new arrival?"

"I think he's trouble." Fallon's voice was flat and hard.

This amused Ezekiel. "Really? And why is that?"

"Sometimes, Zeke, I really wonder if'n you ever been out in the world at all." Fallon looked exasperated. "Going down the same road as Philip, I'll warrant. This Brainerd's set his cap for Anne-Marie. But he's not soft-spoken like Philip was, this feller won't quit. And she's leading him." He shook his head. "She's so willful sometimes. And naïve about people to boot. No idea what kind of man this fella might really be. Thinks the ravens told her it was destiny or some fool thing, for him to show up here."

"Ravens?" Ezekiel raised an eyebrow. "That is interesting, indeed. You know it's entirely possible, Jonas. The ravens do speak to her."

"I know," Fallon admitted. "Might be so. But they're still just goddamn birds. They don't know about people. But I do," he added. "Destiny or not, I can tell when a man rides with trouble. Brainerd's one of those."

"So were you, once." Ezekiel clapped him on the shoulder. "We must not go looking for new quarrels. We shall trust our sister and her ravens for the moment. Think good thoughts, Jonas."

Reluctantly, Jonas nodded.

But he couldn't help thinking that, good thoughts or not, trouble had come looking for them, and he resolved that he would be ready for it when it came.

• • •

"That was when it started to go bad," Fallon told Cheyanne. "That son of a bitch Brainerd was the last fella you'd want—never mind, Lisbet's back." He stood and waved at Doctor Lisbet, who stood just outside the café's front window, holding the reins of both Sultan and of Cheyanne's pony Isobel. "We best get a move on."

"Where are we going?" Cheyanne's voice was torn between nervousness and excitement.

Fallon chuckled. "I guess we're going to go find that son of a bitch Brainerd," he said. "Vile as he is, he's part of this. He's got a connection to Anne-Marie like Lisbet and me. Silver's calling him too, I'm certain sure. We need him."

"Where is he?"

"Good question." Fallon shrugged. "I heard he was up towards the Metolius River country. We'll find him."

"How?"

"Damn if you aren't just full of questions, girl." Fallon laughed, and for once it held real warmth. He reached out and tousled her hair. "I imagine once we're in Metolius territory we'll look around and see who the angry husbands are shootin' at. That's where Brainerd'll be, for certain."

Still snorting with laughter at his own joke, he turned and headed for the door, and Cheyanne had no choice but to follow.

• • •

"We'll find him."

Four

Screams In Silver

Fallon set a brisk pace for them, once they were clear of the settlement. Not enough to overly tax the horses but not dawdling, either. North and east out of Hackett Creek, following it further upstream into the mountains.

Doctor Lisbet rode Sultan, as usual. Cheyanne rode her little paint pony Isobel, and Fallon was on his big bay mare. When Cheyanne asked the bay's name, Fallon blinked. "Hell if I know. Bought it off'n a guy in Canyon City after the one I was on went lame. It's just a horse."

"Horses should have names." Cheyanne was a little scandalized by how casual Fallon was about it.

This amused the man in black. "Well, fine. You come up with a name and I'll try'n remember to use it. Anything for a lady."

So for the next hour or so as they continued along the trail, Cheyanne thought of different names and tried them out. Fallon raised objections to each one of them. Finally Cheyanne realized she was being teased and exploded, "All right, whatever then! Have it your way! Call her Girl Horse! That should be easy enough."

"I already call her girl," Fallon chuckled. "That's easy enough. I guess she does have a name then after all, don't you, Girl?" And he reached down and patted the bay's shoulder.

Doctor Lisbet had remained quiet throughout all of this, but Cheyanne thought she caught an amused glint in her eye. Seeing this, she still felt a little exasperated, but it caused Cheyanne to realize that she kind of enjoyed being teased by the big man. It made her feel like an equal. After all, Fallon often teased Doctor Lisbet as well, though she generally ignored his asides. Apparently it was just how he talked to people.

It was not a well-traveled road, sometimes hardly more than a game trail, but Fallon seemed to know the country. He acted like he was sure of where they were going, though when Cheyanne or Doctor Lisbet asked a specific question he would merely shrug or grunt. Finally Cheyanne pushed her little pony alongside where Doctor Lisbet sat astride Sultan and asked, "Why is he not telling us anything?"

"I think he is listening," Lisbet said. "Something we learned at

Stonegarden. When someone is near that has used the Language, those of us that are attuned to it can sense it."

"Can you do it?"

"I have been trying, a little," the doctor admitted. "But I am out of practice, and it pains me. Jonas, on the other hand, seems much more adept at such things than he was in the old days. I assume this is how he has been tracking all of us."

Cheyanne nodded, not really understanding it but willing to accept Lisbet's word.

The forest around them was largely quiet; Fallon led them along the upper ridges of the mountain, almost to the timberline. They could see the valley spread out below them on the east, turning from green to brown as the forest ended and the desert country began.

On the afternoon of the third day, Doctor Lisbet's patience ran out. Fallon had called a halt, and as Cheyanne gathered kindling from deadfalls laying a little way from the campsite, she heard Lisbet say, "Jonas, this man-of-mystery performance of yours is frankly becoming tiresome. We have stopped for the day and I want to hear more than grunts or acerbic jokes. What are we doing? Is your idea to reunite all of us who studied at that accursed place? Assuming that is even possible, what then? What do you propose that we actually *do*?"

Cheyanne turned and tiptoed closer to where the two were standing. Neither one noticed her.

Fallon sighed heavily and leaned against a boulder. He took the makings out of his shirt pocket and rolled a cigarette. "Lisbet, I don't have answers for you. I know that there is nothing you hate more in the world than bein' disorganized and trying to do things just by guess and by God, but sometimes that's all a fella's got. I swear to you, I don't have a secret plan. I just know what I know. The silver, it's Anne-Marie, she's calling us back. Don't you feel it?"

"I don't—" Lisbet's voice faltered for a moment, then she went on, firmly, "I have tried to suppress it. I avoid using the Language, for reasons that seem to me to be sound and healthy ones. I have been doing my best to move on from that time, Jonas. Are you sure that this… this call you claim to hear, are you certain it isn't just guilt? Or even something else? Something best left ignored," she added. "I thought we had determined that the forces we were meddling with at Stonegarden were not meant for us. The Kuyagah left the runestones as a warning, not an enticement."

Fallon lit his cigarette. He drew deep and then exhaled a plume of white smoke, turning his head so as not to inundate Lisbet with it, and saw Cheyanne standing with her armful of wood. He waved her to join them. "Come on over, Miss Cheyanne. You might as well get your licks in too. What do you say?"

Cheyanne dropped her bundle and began to arrange it into a bed for the fire she was building. "I think it would be nice if you explained some more," she said. "About Anne-Marie."

Fallon raised his eyebrows and looked at Doctor Lisbet, who in turn stared helplessly back at him. She started to say something and then stopped. Fallon snorted. Then, to Cheyanne's consternation, both Fallon and Doctor Lisbet burst out laughing.

"Oh, my dear," Lisbet said, finally. She wiped her eyes. "Explain Anne-Marie? If only we could."

Fallon nodded and his mouth quirked in a wry smile. "I don't think any of us ever understood that girl."

"But it's all about her." Cheyanne was not going to be put off this time. She glared at the tall man. "Why? Why is it her calling you, Mr. Fallon? How are you so sure?"

"I'm not dead sure," Fallon admitted. "You ladies got me there." He considered it. Finally he took off his dark spectacles and looked directly at the two of them with his eerie silver gaze. "Tell you what. You listen with me, Lisbet, and tell me what you think. Miss Cheyanne, you watch, see if her eyes change again. She'll feel it certain, but you can see for yourself as well." He waited. "Well? Lisbet?"

"All right." Doctor Lisbet sighed. "I agree. That is reasonable. Just... be patient. I am not so practiced as you, Jonas."

"Join hands," Fallon instructed. "You too, Miss Cheyanne."

They did so. Fallon whispered something, some kind of phrase that Cheyanne strained to hear but somehow could not quite grasp. *This is the Language*, she realized. She was not really hearing the words so much as feeling them; a charge was building between the three of them as Fallon continued to whisper. *Like the air before a storm.* She started to feel dizzy. She stumbled and would have fallen, when suddenly Lisbet uttered a sharp cry and broke away. She grasped Cheyanne's shoulder and steadied them both.

"You heard that too, Lisbet?" Fallon's voice was clipped and hard.

"Y...yes." Doctor Lisbet was very pale but her jaw was set. "Very well. I suppose you want to ride out now."

Fallon nodded. "Soon. Won't do to ruin the horses. We'll water 'em and let 'em have something to eat, and we'll eat ourselves too. But we won't be making camp just yet. We leave in twenty minutes." Without waiting for a reply he turned and strode over to where the horses were picketed.

Cheyanne was about to boil over with frustrated curiosity. "What are you both talking about? What did you hear?"

"He is telling the truth about Anne-Marie," Lisbet said, tightly. "I heard her too. But more, we heard a psychic cry of mortal fear from Brainerd as well. Much closer. He is facing death. Men with guns. Not far from here. We have little time."

"What are we going to do about men with guns?" Cheyanne heard the slight squeak of fear in her own voice and it embarrassed her. She cleared her throat and added, "I mean, we aren't planning to kill anyone, are we?"

"I trust not." Doctor Lisbet's voice had regained some of its usual asperity. "Certainly not on the behalf of someone as worthless as Nels Brainerd," she added, more to herself than to Cheyanne. "Chances are good that if the man has a posse after him it is for just cause."

"Can't be helped." This was Fallon, returning. "We need him. Here, I got some jerky and some of that dry fruit mix of yours, Lisbet. You'll have to make do till we go extricate that stupid son of a bitch from whatever he's got himself into. Eat up now, and then we ride. Lisbet, you still got that Smith and Wesson you used to carry?"

"I have it, yes. But I haven't fired it in years," Doctor Lisbet replied, her voice rueful. "I don't hunt any more. We rarely eat meat and when we do, it's usually a gift from a grateful patient. I only brought it along out of habit and caution."

"Well, you can wave it around some. Try'n look mean." Fallon winked at Cheyanne and added, "Time was Lisbet's scolding could raise a blister on a fella if she was mad enough."

Despite her fears about what they were embarked on, Cheyanne couldn't help giggling at that; she had to agree it was true.

Doctor Lisbet frowned at both of them and said, "Jonas exaggerates."

"Not by much. You can ask Brainerd, he felt her lash once or twice as I recall. If he's not dead, that is." Fallon wolfed the last of his jerky and shook his head. "Which reminds me that we best mount up. I'll fetch the horses."

As he walked away, Cheyanne glanced at Doctor Lisbet and realized that her guardian's eyes had silvered again. "Your eyes—"

"I know," Lisbet said. She grimaced. "You don't have to say anything. I can feel it."

"But what—"

"Later." Doctor Lisbet held up a hand and sighed. "Assuming there is a later and this rescue of Brainerd doesn't get us all shot. Come on, little one. We need to move or Jonas will be galloping off without us."

Cheyanne wondered if that would be such a bad thing, but she kept it to herself as she followed Lisbet to where Fallon was waiting with the horses.

• • •

They rode as hastily as they dared for the next hour, though their pace was often slowed by the narrow trail and the overhanging trees. Finally the trail emerged into a defile where they could see a small creek at the foot of a ravine, but there was no easy way to move on from that point; the path ended in a steep slope that was beyond the horses.

Then they heard the flat crack of a rifle shot, followed by several more from the other side of the gorge. Fallon straightened and peered down into the ravine. "They got him boxed in, looks like. East side of the ravine, there. Don't see a horse. He's got a rifle, but when his ammo's out he's done."

"That shouldn't be possible." Doctor Lisbet frowned. "With the Language he could escape any number of ways. Why would he allow…?"

"We get him out, we'll ask him," Fallon cut her off. "Right now I'm more interested in shutting down the people chasin' him. Lisbet, you got your gun?"

Doctor Lisbet nodded, her lips thinned in a tight line. She made to hand it to Fallon but he waved it away. "Naw, I don't want it. I just want you to get down there and reason with them fellas whilst I fetch Brainerd. I think they'll more likely listen to you."

"Why not you?" Cheyanne blurted.

Fallon didn't answer right away. Behind his dark spectacles, Cheyanne would have sworn he looked a little ashamed. "Cause I think Lisbet would do a better job of it," he said, his voice curt. "Let's not waste time arguing. Lisbet?"

Doctor Lisbet nodded again and sighed. She slid off Sultan and fished the .32 out of her saddlebags, checked the loads, and tucked it into her waistband.

"All right. Give me a minute or so then you can find your way over to them other shooters." Fallon was off his big bay horse without waiting for a reply. He briefly assessed the ground below one last time, and then went skidding down the muddy slope to where the muzzle flash of the rifle was showing.

"What—" Again Cheyanne had so many questions that she couldn't decide which one to ask first. Before she could say anything, though, Lisbet put a finger to her lips.

"Hush, now." Doctor Lisbet concentrated for a moment, then shook her head. "I can feel Brainerd but he is not using the Language. I think I can cover us with a glamour that will let us approach his attackers, but you must remain close to me. We'll leave Isobel and Sultan here; secure the reins on that branch." She pointed. "Fallon's Girl, too."

Cheyanne dismounted and did as Lisbet asked. Then she returned to where the doctor stood, staring at nothing, her brow deeply furrowed. Cheyanne could see her lips moving, but no sound came. Instead, Cheyanne felt the eerie charge building in the air again.

Abruptly Doctor Lisbet turned to her and said, "Take my hand."

Cheyanne did so.

Then Lisbet turned and stepped off the edge of the ravine into mid-air over the slope. Pulling Cheyanne with her.

Cheyanne could not have described the sensation. They were moving rapidly, but not falling. Instead, they were gliding above the dirt and pebbles that sloped down to the bottom of the defile, leaving no trace, almost… like how a water bug moved over the surface of a lake. That was all Cheyanne could think of.

As they approached the bottom of the slope Lisbet released Cheyanne and their feet sank to the ground. When they were standing normally again Cheyanne realized she had been holding her breath and took a deep, shuddering inhale.

Doctor Lisbet flashed her a reassuring smile, then pulled out her .32 and motioned for Cheyanne to stay behind her. They could see three men ahead of them, barricaded behind a tumble of boulders.

One of them stood and snapped off a shot where they had seen Fallon going. "Somebody else is up there with him," he grunted.

"Your problem isn't him, it's me."

The three of them whirled to see Doctor Lisbet covering them with her Smith and Wesson. "Drop your iron, gentlemen."

"The hell!" The one holding the rifle started to raise it, then stopped. "Your eyes," he muttered. "Look at her eyes—just like—"

"Never mind my eyes. It's my pistol that should concern you." Lisbet said this with easy confidence, using the same brisk tone Cheyanne had heard her use a thousand times with recalcitrant patients in Hackett Creek. "I have no quarrel with you but we need that worthless skunk you are chasing. Whatever you want him for, our need is greater."

"What's he done to you? Are you his kin?" This was an older man, standing just behind the one with the rifle. He shouldered his way forward and spat. "Or his woman, mebbe? You should know he was caught with Lanny Barker's wife and when Lanny took exception to it he up and shot him dead right there in the man's own bedroom. He'll hang for murder. We are lawful deputies pursuing a criminal."

Lisbet eyed the man. "Are you the sheriff, then?"

"Lanny was the sheriff." This was the third, a boy of no more than fifteen. "I'm his son and these two are his brothers. I don't want no shootout with a lady, but we have a right to this man of your'n and we aim to take him. There's three of us and two of you and you are womenfolk."

"We are still dangerous." Cheyanne heard the edge in Doctor Lisbet's voice and hid a smile. The boy had said exactly the wrong thing as far as Lisbet was concerned. "Do not test me."

"Come on, don't make this—" the oldest Barker began, but then the younger brother with the rifle lunged forward, making a wild grab for Lisbet's pistol. He was barely a yard away from them yet somehow, impossibly, he passed –through? alongside? Cheyanne couldn't tell—from where they were standing to loop around and land sprawled face-first in the mud exactly where he had started from. Lisbet's lips were moving silently again and Cheyanne could feel the building charge of the Language. Then she stepped forward and raised a hand, pointing at each of the three men in succession.

"You lost his trail an hour ago," Lisbet said, her voice sounding eerie and layered upon itself. *"You have no memory of us, we were never here. You will return whence you came and bury your dead.* Say yes if you understand."

There was a muttered chorus of agreement from the three. Lisbet waited a moment, then, satisfied, tucked her pistol back into her waistband and nodded at Cheyanne to join her. She held out her hand. Cheyanne took it and together they began to glide back up the slope to where the horses were tied.

Suddenly Cheyanne felt a flare of pain shoot up her arm from where her hand clasped Doctor Lisbet's. They both fell, but fortunately they were only a few inches from the top. Cheyanne scrambled up to the edge and held out a hand, which Lisbet took thankfully. Once Doctor Lisbet was safely over the top, the two just sat panting helplessly on the ground for a moment, not caring about the muddy state of their attire.

"I am sorry, little one." Cheyanne saw that Lisbet's eyes were shining an even brighter silver than before, and then realized it was because they were swimming with tears. "I haven't attempted anything like that in almost a decade. It's a miracle I didn't drop us sooner. We might have broken our necks."

Cheyanne said, hesitantly, "You were amazing."

Doctor Lisbet's answering smile was wan. "It was mostly bluff. But I have learned a little about talking to stubborn men after ten years of doctoring in Hackett Creek." She shook her head. "Jonas was not exaggerating. Opening myself fully to the Hermetic perceptions again, allowing myself to see and hear—" She shivered. "I sensed it only partially before. Then, I thought it was merely an echo from that last terrible night, from the fire. But this is happening now. It is impossible to ignore her. The screaming. She is desperate. Abandoned. Terrified. For herself and also for us. It is nearly unbearable. I can hear her even now."

"Anne-Marie?"

Doctor Lisbet could only nod. "If this is what Jonas hears all the time…" she whispered. "His urgency is clear to me now. It might drive a man mad. Help me stand."

Together they struggled to their feet. Lisbet looked at Cheyanne's muddy and bedraggled figure and then glanced down at her own clothing, which was just as bad. "Frontier living," she muttered. "Oh well."

There was a commotion from the woods and they both turned to see Fallon dragging a bulky figure by the collar of his woolen jacket. He heaved the man forward to land in a sprawl at the feet of the two women.

"Nels Brainerd, ladies," Fallon gasped. He glared at the man lying on the ground. "Now stay still, you stupid son of a bitch, or I'll hit you again."

Slowly the man sat up and rubbed his face. His hair was an odd mixture of blond and white, streaked in such a way that it seemed to shimmer in the late afternoon light. He dropped his hand to his side and stared at the three of them with unblinking silver eyes.

"Who the hell are you?" he asked.

● ● ●

Five

Other Men's Wives (Brainerd's Story)

For a moment the three of them could only stare at the blond man. Finally Fallon sputtered, "For Chrissakes, I didn't hit you that hard. You know who we are."

Doctor Lisbet shook her head. "I don't think he does, Jonas. Look at his aura. There is no deceit there." She paused. "Jonas… I washed clean the memories of his attackers. I haven't tried anything like that since we were at the abbey; it's possible that in my clumsiness—"

"Naw." Fallon's brow furrowed. Behind his dark spectacles Cheyanne could see he was squinting in puzzled appraisal of the man before them. "You got it that wrong, we'd all of us be wandering around the woods with no memory wondering what the hell. Somebody wiped him clean, though, for certain." He leaned forward and addressed Brainerd directly. "No recollection of us at all? Not me nor Lisbet nor the abbey? Nothing?"

Brainerd shook his head. He scrambled to his feet and rubbed his jaw. "I'd remember you, mister," he said. "I'll sure remember today. You can have the one punch because you apparently took that posse off my back but you only get the one, understand?" His gaze turned to Doctor Lisbet and Cheyanne, really looking at them for the first time. He brightened. "Hello to you, ladies," he added, and tipped his hat. "Pleasure to see such pretty girls out here in the middle of nowheres."

"Oh, for heaven's sake." Lisbet rolled her eyes. "Clearly you have learned nothing in the last decade. We are tired and sweaty and covered in mud, but still, nevertheless, any time you see a woman you think of nothing but—well. I see we are going to have to start all over. I said ten years ago that if you *ever* come near me I will geld you like a horse, I have the skills and the surgical tools to do it, and it would be an act of mercy to the women of the American West. It's still true and that goes double for this young lady, who is under my protection. Do you understand?"

Brainerd scowled. "I was just bein' polite. No need—"

"Shut up." This was Fallon. "You got a horse?"

"Yonder." Brainerd pointed. His voice was sulky. "I think I been more than tolerant but it's about time for us to part ways. You all—" His voice trailed off. "That horse there. The big black. Him, I know." He squinted at Sultan, just behind where Cheyanne was standing. "From somewhere. Desert country. It was… damn it. I lost it."

"Anne-Marie," Cheyanne said, suddenly. "Do you remember Anne-Marie?"

Slowly, Brainerd nodded. Cheyanne would have sworn the silver in his eyes had flared a little at the name. "Little blonde girl. Tease. Knew her… a long time ago."

"Do you hear her?" Fallon took off his spectacles, revealing his own silvered eyes. "As we do?"

Brainerd nodded, again. "Hear something," he mumbled. "Whispers. Ringin' in my ears. Thought it was just m'hangover. What is that, in your eyes… and hers too? What in…"

"Your eyes show silver the same as ours do. It's why we came for you." Doctor Lisbet turned to Fallon. "Can you restore his memories?"

"Not by m'self. Together we might." The tall man straightened and looked at Brainerd with appraisal. "What about it, Nels? Don't you ever wonder what you were doing in the desert ten years gone?"

"I know what I was doing," Brainerd said, defensive. "I was—" His face clouded. "I was…" He stopped. "The hell? What are you people doing to me?" A note of fear crept into his voice. "What's wrong with your eyes, anyway? Why can't I remember? Who *are* you?"

"We spent time in the desert, years ago. Fetch your horse and follow us and we'll explain it all." Fallon pointed. "Best hurry. Them fellas chasin' you won't be a problem for a while but they might have had friends."

Brainerd considered it, frowning, then finally nodded. "All right. But you and me ain't done, mister. You'll regret the day you crossed me."

"Already do," Fallon replied, grinning. "Have for years, actually. You have no idea. But we need you, so mount up and let's go."

• • •

The sun was setting when Fallon finally called a halt. "I guess this'll do."

They had descended along the ravine another couple of miles, where it opened out into a small wooded valley. They dismounted, picketed the horses, and while Cheyanne gathered more deadfalls for a fire, the others unpacked their bedrolls and cleared a small place for a fire pit.

This was not the same kind of forest around Hackett Creek, but thinner and sparser, with the thick fir and pine Cheyanne was used to seeing giving way to larch and juniper. The ground itself had a reddish cast. She asked Doctor Lisbet about it.

"Higher clay content," Lisbet replied, crisply. "It means we are getting closer to desert country. The red layering is what gave the Painted Desert its name."

"Where are we now?"

"East of Sisters. About halfway to the Ochocos." This was Fallon. "There's a wagon track about a mile yonder, but we came the back way, on account of our friend here." He nodded at Brainerd and spat. "Takes a special kind of stupid, killing a lawman over a piece of ass. Hope she was worth it."

"Not really." Brainerd shrugged. "Fella drew on me. It was a fair fight, and anyways she never said she was married."

"That doesn't mean you didn't know she was." Doctor Lisbet's look was severe. "As I recall, though, that sort of thing never bothered you."

The blond man glared. "You people talk like you know me, but I don't know you from nothing. I thought you said you were gonna explain. Well, get to it."

Fallon looked over at Lisbet. Reluctantly, she nodded and turned back to Brainerd. "Someone took your memory," she said. "We are going to try and give it back to you. Through a kind of... hypnosis, let's say. Have you heard of this?"

"What, like staring at a watch fob till you make me quack like a duck?" Brainerd made a face. "No thanks. If that's all you got, I'll just—" His voice trailed off and his head drooped forward a little. Abruptly he sat on the ground, his head rolling bonelessly.

Cheyanne realized that Fallon had been whispering the Language while Lisbet was talking to Brainerd. He straightened and grinned at the two of them over Brainerd's inert form. "Been wanting to shut him up like that since the day I met him."

Doctor Lisbet managed a small smile, though Cheyanne could see she was nervous. "Very well, Jonas. How do you propose we do this?"

"Forced trance, truth-telling. Like that time with Larry. Only this time—"

Lisbet held up a hand and winced. "Don't remind me." At Cheyanne's inquiring look, she added, "A tale for another time. I must concentrate." She took a deep breath. "Jonas and I will be unresponsive for a while. Do not be alarmed. We are going to be trying to reach Brainerd's buried memory. Just keep watch for now. Don't try to rouse us."

Cheyanne nodded. Lisbet turned to Jonas and they moved silently to where Brainerd sat. Jonas took Lisbet's hand.

"Where shall we begin?" Lisbet's voice was shaking, just a little, Cheyanne noticed.

"Where it always does." Fallon was grim. "With Anne-Marie."

● ● ●

Brainerd had run to the desert because of a woman—well, really, the woman's husband, who had not taken kindly to the arrangement Brainerd had made with his missus—and now he had decided to stay because of one. He grimaced. Well, at least this girl wasn't married.

She sure was maddening, though. Always just out of reach. Anne-Marie genuinely liked him, though, he could tell. Not like that bitch doctor always buried in her books. The one time he'd sidled up to Lisbet and put an arm around her she'd rocked him with a slap that damn near dislocated his jaw. Normally after something like that he'd have clouted her back and taught her some manners, but things were different at Stonegarden. The rules about people seemed different than what he'd grown up with, and anyway that lady doctor knew enough Language to scramble his innards good if she'd taken a notion to do it. So he let it go. It was mostly just habit that had led him to try, anyway, like scratching an itch.

It was Anne-Marie that obsessed him.

Nelson Brainerd had a way with women, always had. Some might have called it charm, but that quality had little to do with it; Brainerd's successes were because of something lower, an animal quality. Lots of the women he'd been with didn't seem to like him much but they still had given themselves to him. And Brainerd himself never said no, naturally.

Though there were times he probably should have. There had been a couple of bad scenes with fathers and husbands like the one that had sent him skedaddling into the desert in the first place, not to mention a couple of ladies caught pregnant and that kind of thing. Some women even whined at him about maybe settling down. There was no way no-how Brainerd was going to stick around for anything like that. House and family and chores was his idea of hell, that was why he'd lit out west in the first place. Maybe his brothers in Wichita liked being on the farm living a life of digging in the dirt like a root hog but not Nelson, no way no-how. He liked to ride and shoot and drink and most nights he liked a willing woman. That simple. The second one of them girls got moony-eyed about making something permanent with a house a-crawling with a lot of kids, he was gone. There was always the next town, the next saloon, and usually there was a next woman to go with them.

Married ones were the best. They knew how to pleasure a man and they usually were more skittish of anything permanent than even he was. Brainerd had gotten good at sizing up which ones weren't getting what they needed at home. It was rare that he couldn't work out a nice little arrangement that benefited both himself and the lady. After a while he'd move on, no regrets. Tidy, like.

Despite his usual habits, though, he'd been here at Stonegarden almost two months with no drinking, no sex, no nothing. Because of this girl Anne-Marie. If Brainerd had been given to introspection he would have been ruefully surprised at how easily he had changed his ways, just to remain near the blonde girl with the easy laugh. He might have even wondered at the power she held over him.

But he was not an introspective man. He only knew that he wanted her. Sometimes he thought about just grabbing her and taking her, the same way he had that little redhead in Boise who'd teased him once too often, or that breed squaw in Hyacinth who wouldn't look at him when he talked to her.

Somehow, though, he could not make himself do it.

The rules were different here. Even a man like Brainerd was able to grasp that. Hell, you only had to see them two sissyboys Larry and Theo holding hands out in front of God and everyone, or that Negro cook Aaron laughing with an old Rebel boy like Jonas Fallon like there had never been no nevermind between North and South at all. That was all fine and well, Brainerd didn't give a damn about that, but the way they let the womenfolk roam around doing whatever the hell they pleased, beholden to no man... He was never going to get used to that.

But none of it really mattered. Anne-Marie, though. She mattered. He wanted her. He wanted her bad. She wanted him too, he was sure. So what was the problem?

• • •

"*Dear Lord, Jonas. I had no idea. His thoughts... it feels like reaching into a basket of snakes.*"

"*I know. But it's got to be done. We always knew what he was after, this*" *is just confirming it. We need to know what happened to his memories. The day before the fire. Push him to that."*

• • •

Brainerd liked to ride and so did Anne-Marie, and in the late afternoon the two of them would often take the horses up to the top of the ridge overlooking the canyon. There was a tiny spring about three-quarters of a mile up from the abbey where they would stop and water the horses. Usually they'd sit for a while and gaze out over the canyon, and sometimes Anne-Marie would let him kiss her, but never anything more. When he reached for her breast she moved away.

"I can't, sweetie."

"Why not?" Brainerd heard the hoarse need in his own voice and it angered and shamed him. "What's the matter with me?"

"I just can't." Her eyes filled with tears. "Don't… just don't ask me."

"You with someone else? Fallon? Ezekiel? They don't have to know. No one does." It had worked a thousand times. That was what women needed, Brainerd knew, the assurance of secrecy.

"It's not like that." She shook her head. "I can't explain."

"But—" Abruptly his mind fogged and when he could see clearly again, both she and Sultan were gone.

Brainerd swore and stood up. He retrieved his horse and rode back to the abbey, where he found Anne-Marie laughing gaily with the others as though nothing had happened. *And nothing had,* he reflected, grimly. But it would. One of these days. He was wearing her down.

At the evening meal he noticed that Anne-Marie was having difficulty meeting his eyes, and then she disappeared shortly afterwards. Brainerd had every intention of following her and pressing his suit again, but Fallon stopped him. "Hey Nels, come on out to the stables with me, I need you to help me with a horse threw a shoe."

"Ask Larry. Or Theo." Brainerd was looking past him, trying to see where the girl had gone.

"I'm asking you." Fallon scowled. "Don't make me ask again."

Brainerd glared back at the tall man but did not argue further. There would come a reckoning with Fallon, he promised himself that, but he knew that Anne-Marie loved him like a brother and Brainerd did not want any bad blood between him and Fallon to scuttle his chances with her. Once he had taken the girl for himself, there would be time for settling scores. Fallon, that bitch doctor, maybe even that little whore back in Canyon City whose husband had chased him out here in the first place. For a moment Brainerd luxuriated in the thought, then followed the other man out to the stable.

The horse turned out to be Sultan. "Hold him still, I gotta trim this a little," Fallon directed Brainerd. He held the hoof with one hand as Fallon deftly shaved away with the nippers.

"You didn't need me for this," Brainerd said. "It's not a two-man job."

Fallon did not answer right away but tapped the shoe into place. He stood. "Maybe not. Maybe I just wanted a word. Man to man."

Well, Brainerd had known it was coming sooner or later. Might as well be tonight. "Yeah?" He released Sultan and the big black moved back into his stall. "Speak your piece then."

"You ain't here for the studying, nor the power," Fallon said. He crossed his arms and leaned against the wooden pillar. "You're here for the girl. I'm telling you for your own good, it's not gonna happen."

"Who's gonna stop me? You?" Brainerd spat. "What makes it your business anyhow?"

"Not my business. Not really." Fallon's smile was thin and rueful. "But people are going to get hurt. Thinking it might be already happening. You're only here because Anne-Marie took a shine to you. But it's not what you think it is."

"How do you know what I 'think' it is?"

"Seriously?" Fallon snorted. "I don't need to see no aura to be able to tell what you are. You are about as subtle as a boar in rut, boy. I imagine you're hell on barmaids and farmer's daughters from here to Colorado, but Anne-Marie's different. She will play you like a fiddle. She's doing it now." At Brainerd's expression, he added, "She used the Language on you, you damn fool. From the beginning, with the ravens. They led you here, didn't they?"

"Just birds," Brainerd's voice was thick and heavy. "Don't mean nothing."

"You know better," Fallon snapped. "Listen to what I am telling you. She's using it all the time now. On herself, the horses, everything. It's dangerous. She's like a kid playing with matches. You dumbass, I'm tryin' to *help* you," he added at Brainerd's expression. "You need to get the hell away from here before she scrambles your brains so bad you never get your head right again."

Brainerd shook his head slowly and glared at Fallon. But in his head a tiny voice was whispering, *Could it be true?* Had he been lured here? Why?

"You don't need me for this..."

"Why aren't you talking to her about this?" Brainerd asked at last.

"I imagine Zeke's talking to her now. I thought it'd be best if I gave you the word before he gets to you." Fallon sighed. "Don't know why I bothered. I guess I figured maybe if you had a chance to talk, away from her, then maybe you might see sense."

"But—" Brainerd rubbed his forehead, as though doing so might force his brain to work better. "But I been studyin' the Language too. I ain't got much but I ought to be able to—"

"All of us are little school kids compared to Zeke and Anne-Marie. They been at this for years." Fallon's smile was pitying. "You never had a chance."

"But... why?" Brainerd's thoughts were swirling with anger and shame and, damn it, the blind desire for the girl. Still. "What could be the reason...?"

"No idea. Probably not good though. Something's going bad here, more'n just Anne-Marie taking you for a turn round the corral. I think Zeke's playing us all like fiddles, same as the girl played you. He found a bunch of us that was all broken and gave us what we wanted, but it's gone sour somehow. Couldn't rightly put a name to it, but the more I learn, the more I think he's hiding some important piece." Fallon spread his hands. "Just trying to be honest with you. Way I figure it we're riding blind and I don't think it's gonna turn out good for any of us. Fact is, I'm thinking it might be time to pull out m'self. I'm going with Lisbet tomorrow." He nodded at the horses. "But if'n I was you I wouldn't wait. Get out now, Nels. While you can."

He did not wait for Brainerd to answer but instead turned and walked back up the path to the cabins.

For a moment Brainerd just stood, his hands knotting into fists until his knuckles were white. Get out hell. He was going to have this out with the little bitch tease. Right now.

● ● ●

"There. We are coming up to it, Jonas. The gap."

"I see it. Like... some kind of gold fog. Can you get under that?"

"Help me. It's fragmented. I can't... Anne-Marie is screaming again. I can only—"

● ● ●

Fragments. Flashes. Memories, Fallon's and Lisbet's and Brainerd's, intermingled and broken. Moments tumbling in a cascade of golden glass.

...the bearded man is laughing. Mocking. There is another figure, red and leathery, with no eyes...

..."Don't argue with me! Take Sultan and get as far away as you can!"

...the girl is weeping over a body on the path.

...The horses are screaming. Sultan is gone. Fire. Fire everywhere.

...the bearded man is pointing. At him? No. Who? "...defiler! You've ruined everything. How dare you..."

...*"I'm sorry, Jonas. I cannot. It* hurts." Lisbet suddenly collapsed, her head in her hands. "All I can hear is the screaming."

Fallon nodded. He looked haggard and shaken. "Did it work?" he asked, roughly.

Brainerd started and sat up straight. He looked up at Lisbet and Fallon and let out a deep, shuddering sigh.

"I remember," he said. "Not all of it, but enough."

Lisbet wiped her eyes.

Fallon looked down at the blond man. "Well? What about it, Nels?"

Brainerd took a long look at the two of them, then at Cheyanne, who stood back a little, wide-eyed. He sighed again. "All right. I'm with you."

Six
Lavender Thistlewine (Larry's Story)

The following morning Doctor Lisbet insisted that they delay moving on long enough for her to wash out their muddied clothing from the day before. "Cheyanne, you and Jonas should take this time to find us some further provisions. There might well be roots and herbs in the woods. Jonas, she knows what to look for, she has accompanied me on these gathering expeditions for years."

"Rabbit food." Brainerd made a face. "I'm gonna see if I can get me some meat. You all can go on and dig like dogs." He rose and moved off into the trees without further comment.

Cheyanne looked at Fallon. He shrugged. "Fine with me. Let's go, Miss Cheyanne."

She followed him into the trees, noting that he chose a different direction than Brainerd. "Why don't you carry a gun? Yesterday you wouldn't even take Doctor Lisbet's, and those men were shooting at you."

"Don't like 'em."

When she saw he was going to leave it at that, Cheyanne pressed him. "But you were in the War."

"That's why I don't like 'em."

This time Cheyanne let it pass. After a few more minutes of trudging over the soft carpet of pine needles and dried juniper covering the forest floor, the silence became awkward. Finally Fallon said, "I found out that I couldn't do it, that's all. Killin. Not even animals. Not after the war. Made m'self sick. So I buy dried meat when I'm in a town and get by on that and bread and cheese. Root vegetables once in a while but that's more Lisbet's style, she's the one used to lecture us on eating all healthful and so on. But me, I like meat fine, I just don't hunt m'own." He quirked an eyebrow at her from behind his dark spectacles. "You don't carry a gun either."

"We trade for our meat mostly," Cheyanne admitted. "This is my first time traveling like this. Camping, I mean."

"Liking it so far?" Fallon grinned. "We're a fun bunch of broken-down old folks for you to be roughing it with, first time out."

She knew he was teasing again, but Cheyanne answered him seriously. "Matter of fact is I am enjoying it," she admitted with some surprise. "I'm scared of what is ahead and I wish we were traveling for some other reason, but... I don't know. I feel more alive. More involved. I don't know, I can't explain it."

"More grownup," Fallon observed. "Never saw a youngster yet wasn't in a hurry to be all adult. Adulthood ain't that much fun, you know."

"It's not that." Cheyanne flushed. It was, maybe. A little. But it was also feeling like Doctor Lisbet was finally unbending a little, sharing more of herself. More like...

"You weren't sure Lisbet thought you were really family before," Fallon said. At her expression, he chuckled. "Girl, you are an open book. You got an aura that sparkles."

"I don't know what you mean," Cheyanne said. "About auras. You all keep talking about it but I have no idea what it is. Is that something you learned at Stonegarden? Like Language?"

"It's all part of it," Fallon stopped and took off his hat and whacked it against his thigh to knock off the needles that had fallen on the brim. "The Language… it's not the words, it ain't like a magic spell or some such. Learning it, using it…it changes the way your brain and eyes work. All living things, they got light coming off 'em. Colors. After a while you can see 'em. It's not like the regular colors you know, not bright like paint or nothing, they don't look colorful exactly, but you start seeing them once… well, when learning the Language changes you enough, I guess."

"Why is Doctor Lisbet afraid of using the Language?" Cheyanne leaned forward. "Why does it hurt her and not you?"

"Because you get to where you can see other things as well as auras." Fallon grunted and put his hat back on. "And they ain't pretty. Anyways, I never said it don't hurt to use it. Sometimes it hurts a lot."

"Like with Larry? The time Doctor Lisbet doesn't want to talk about?"

"Yes. Like that." Fallon shook his head and grinned again. "You are persistent, girl."

"You knew I would ask, though." Cheyanne grinned back at him. "Didn't you? Doesn't my sparkling aura tell you already? You might as well tell me."

Fallon gave her a long look, sighed, and nodded. "Might as well."

● ● ●

The daily routine at Stonegarden was relatively simple. There was no set schedule, but it was generally understood that mornings were for study. They were up with the sunrise, and after a morning meal Ezekiel would go to the runestones and the obsidian pool, laboriously working to copy down the markings on the stones. Sometimes Lisbet or Lawrence would accompany him but it was difficult for any of them other than Ezekiel to look upon the markings themselves for any length of time. Lisbet especially found it dizzying and if she was not careful she would be sidelined for the rest of the day with a crippling headache. Most of the time they were content to work with Ezekiel's transcriptions to do their translating work. Lawrence and Lisbet were the best at it; both had orderly minds and Lisbet, especially, had a knack for seeing the underlying structure of the Kuyagah's linguistic style. The two of them formed a habit of hunkering down with their papers in Lisbet's cabin of a morning—it was roomier than the one Lawrence shared with Theo, and the table was wider—and working on pages of transcribed runes together.

"You have to let go of the Latin forms," she told Lawrence. "They don't use words the same way at all. No European language works this way. The Kuyagah's interpretation of human sensory experience is literally different than anything any other language is built on. There is no one-to-one transliteration possible here; their word for rocks is the same as the one for water. Their concept of anything that we might refer to with a noun structure is malleable and temporary. They do not differentiate between things that are material and things we would regard as ethereal or even nonexistent. It is not a cypher. This is not decoding."

"When you say things like that, you make it sound impossible," Lawrence sighed and leaned back in his chair. "How did Ezekiel get as far as he did with no one here but himself and that twitterpated girl?"

"He is a brilliant man, undoubtedly." Lisbet's tone was somewhat guarded. The truth was that she herself often had wondered this, especially after finding out that most of the group had been there less than two years. "Once he made the initial breakthrough, it would not have been that difficult to carry on. I can follow his work easily enough. Anne-Marie is brilliant in her own way as well, despite the façade she presents. The linguistic study is not difficult once we have the key that Ezekiel has provided. But employing the Language to influence one's surroundings... that is extraordinarily difficult for you and me, but that twitterpated girl you are dismissing does it with ease."

"Too much ease." Lawrence thinned his lips in distaste. "I sometimes think she is using it as the old Chinamen in San Francisco use opium, to live in dreams for weeks on end. Did you notice that she has the golden glow upon her almost all the time now?"

"We use the Language as well. The glow is upon us from time to time. Certainly it is not physically harmful to the body as an opiate would be. Rather the opposite, if anything. I owe my life to it, remember." Lisbet frowned. "You sound so judgmental, all of a sudden. Do you disapprove of the work we are doing here?"

"I don't know." Lawrence shrugged. "Does it matter? I'm here for my reasons, and Theo is for his. Come for the refuge, stay for the power. You obviously are here for the healing properties of the Language but I think there is more to it for you as well, isn't there?"

"Everyone has their own reasons for everything." Startled, they both turned to see Fallon smiling at them from the door of the cabin. "Lunchtime, kids. Aaron's somehow conjured up a stew and even a couple of pies that would win a prize at the fair, I think. And he don't use the Language doing it far's I can tell."

"You move like a cat," Lawrence said, looking faintly annoyed. "Were you listening in to all that?"

"Heard some." Fallon shrugged. "Sorry if I made you nervous."

Lawrence was nervous, Lisbet saw; inexplicably so. She wondered why. She said as much to Fallon as they made their way to where Theo and Aaron were setting up lunch at the outdoor line of tables just before the path leading to the abbey building.

Fallon shook his head. "Never can tell with Larry. He's like a big cat his own self sometimes. Changeable. He'll be purring right along and then turn and claw you just out of pure cussedness. Usually Theo can smooth him over, or Anne-Marie. You can't argue with him though or he'll just dig in."

"Well, he certainly seems prickly today."

"Ever'body's prickly lately," Fallon said. "Zeke too. Ever since Philip took off couple months back. Kinda threw everybody." He sighed. "Sometimes I wonder if it's just going bad here, Lisbet. Maybe we expected too much."

"Too much how?" Lisbet's brow narrowed. "What expectations did you have? I thought you were the one that got along with everyone."

"That was it." Fallon's smile was almost sad. "I expected we'd all always get along. That we'd be… better. But I guess that was too much. Sooner or later, people get testy and quarrelsome. That's just natural, I guess, even when you are doing unnatural work." He chuckled sourly at that, and spread his hands. "Oh, don't mind me, gorgeous. Certainly isn't the first time Larry's been snitty for no reason and it won't be the last. Let's go eat."

But Lisbet did not smile. The thought stayed with her throughout the afternoon. The powers they were exploring… if applied with the caprices of human frailty, the results could be dangerous indeed. They *had* to be better. They dared be no less.

• • •

Often, in the evenings, the group gathered around a big campfire in the center of the clearing where the cabins stood. Occasionally they shared around a jug of herbal liquor that was a recipe that Theo and Lawrence had brought with them from Idaho. Fallon, the seasoned drinker of the group, suggested that the primary ingredients must have been lavender, thistles, and donkey piss but still took his share. The comment made Lawrence flush angrily but Theo laughed heartily and said, "Our secret is out!" which made the entire group collapse in hysterics.

Ezekiel usually eschewed these informal campfire sessions, and so he usually ended up being the primary subject of speculation.

"How'd you know to even find this place at all?" Fallon asked Anne-Marie one night. "Was you and Ezekiel riding up this way for a reason?"

"I think it was destiny," Anne-Marie said. "I think we were all meant to be here. Don't you? It feels so natural, all of us being here, in this place, laughing together."

"I felt that when I first arrived," Lisbet admitted. "Nels too, I think."

"Sure ain't natural for me to be without a drink for weeks on end," Brainerd said. "Pass me that jug of lavender slop, boy." Theo handed it to him and he took a deep draught, then licked his lips. "Ain't so bad once you get used to it."

"Ain't a real drink, though," Fallon said. "Not like real sippin whiskey."

"How would you know?" Lawrence was smiling but there was bite in the words. "I didn't think they allowed men of your sort in the kind of gentlemen's club where one finds quality liquor."

"You'd be surprised." Fallon smiled back, but his eyes were sad. "Dad used to swing a pretty wide loop in Chicago. I been to one or two of them clubs you're talking about." He snorted. "Got asked to leave pretty quick though. Not a place to do serious drinking."

"You mean like with a brawl and vomiting at the end?" Lawrence's tone was light but his eyes were hard. "I thought Chicago was a rough town."

"You don't want to see a rough town, boy." This was Brainerd. "Not for real. They'd take you n'Theo here for a ride you wouldn't forget in a hurry."

"Oh, don't quarrel, boys." Anne-Marie's smile, as usual, defused the growing unease. "Let's talk about something nice. Frowning makes wrinkles."

Even Brainerd smiled a little at that. "Well, fine, kitten. What do you think we should talk about?"

"Secrets," the blonde girl responded brightly. "We'll go round the circle and each tell their darkest secret. Then there won't be any reason for anyone to feel uncomfortable again ever."

"Ha!" Fallon snorted. "You first then, youngster."

"All right." Anne-Marie did not look at all perturbed at the prospect. She took a deep breath and said, "I am afraid I'll never be loved."

"The hell?" Fallon was the one to blurt it out loud, but the whole group looked taken aback. "You're loco. Everyone loves you."

"Everyone *likes* me," Anne-Marie corrected him. "But no one thinks I'm serious ever. I long for… real love, like in books. Romance. Passion."

Though they tried not to be obvious about it, Lawrence, Fallon, and Lisbet could not keep themselves from glancing over at Brainerd. He was very pale and his lips worked a little, but no words came out.

Anne-Marie pointedly ignored him. "That's mine. Lisbet?"

Lisbet opened her mouth to say she did not care to participate, but what came out was, "I don't like people. Not really. I became a doctor because I enjoy science and study but I fear I am not very good at the actual healing. I think I might have become just another dried-up old academic if not for the journey that led me here. You are the first real friends I have ever had and even so, it is difficult for me to talk to you all. It shames me and I don't know why." She swallowed and realized that her eyes were swimming with tears. She looked helplessly over at Fallon.

Fallon said thickly, "I'm scared of Ezekiel. I'm scared of the Language. I think what we do here is gonna end badly. I think I regret the devil's bargain I made with the old man and... what the hell!" He glared at Anne-Marie and gritted, "You did this. Di'... *something* to us. What? What did you do?"

"She enchanted the wine," Lawrence said, his voice bitter. "She did something to the wine..."

"I made it so you can't lie," Anne-Marie said. "Nor me either. None of us can from now until morning. We should have no secrets." She smiled at Lawrence. "Your turn, Larry. Confess now. Your darkest secret."

Lawrence looked murderously at her but what he said was, "Love and passion? That's what you want? All right then, you little bitch, I don't love Theo any more. If I ever did. I love Ezekiel, and he loves you, and none of us can have what we want. How's that, you evil little strumpet? Happy now? You'll have to settle for this rough-hewn playmate your damn birds brought." He waved vaguely at Brainerd.

Brainerd looked as though he might go for his gun but Fallon said, "Whoa. That's enough, all of you. Let this all go now afore someone gets hurt."

"Someone's already hurt, you great lumbering clod," Lawrence snapped. "That's what happens when you take secrets away. Secrets and lies are the bandages we put over the hurt. And this little girl tore them all off. Why? For fun? To see us all squirm?"

Anne-Marie abruptly stood and ran up the path to the abbey. Brainerd and Fallon both stood to go after her but Lawrence stopped them. "Let her go. Maybe it's best for all of us if she confronts the old man. Go to bed and sleep this off. Forget it." He looked sorrowfully at Theo and added, "I don't know how to—"

"Forget it," Theo said. His voice was clipped. "I already knew, you fool. I knew weeks ago but I pretend not to. That's *my* dark secret."

There was silence for a moment.

"Sort it out later," Fallon said, finally. His voice was thick and bleary. He stood. "Just… Call it a night. Tomorrow's a fresh start."

"I agree," Lisbet said, shakily. "My sight is blurred and I am unsure if I can manage even the few steps to the cabin. Perhaps… perhaps we should just put it down to the wine, gentlemen."

● ● ●

"And we did," Fallon told Cheyanne. "Next day we all went about our business like normal and it *was* normal. Mostly. But that night, for a second there—I could see everyone's thoughts and they saw mine. And they was ugly. Pain, regret. Things like that. Everyone looked… broken. I knew it and they all knew it too. We got a glimpse inside each other and it wasn't the pretty picture we'd painted for ourselves." He took a deep, shuddering breath and let it out slowly. "Spooked us all. Next night was the fire. Still not sure how it happened but I am sure it was that session with the wine that lit the fuse. Set off Larry, Nels, even Lisbet. For whatever devilish reason, Anne-Marie primed us all that night for some kind of showdown."

Cheyanne waited. When the tall man said nothing further, she asked, "A showdown. With Ezekiel, do you think?"

"Maybe. Maybe she was trying to get shucked of him and needed us all to help. But… she could have just asked us for that. Hell, Brainerd asked her to ride off with him more than once, I'm certain sure. I don't know. I don't know anything any more. I thought they was dead. Till the silver came."

"Are we having the showdown now? Is that what we're riding into?"

"If I knew I'd tell you, girl. I guess we won't know till we get where we're going." Fallon sighed again. "Come on, Miss Cheyanne, let's find some grub. You show me the healthy stuff Lisbet likes."

Cheyanne nodded and moved ahead of the man in black, but her mind was not on plants. She was wondering about Stonegarden, and secrets, and destiny.

● ● ●

Seven
The Silver Riders Come

Two days' further ride brought them to the end of the forest country. The grass was sparse and the trees looked dry and scraggly; little more than "weeds with ambition," as Fallon remarked with his usual sardonic expression.

Fallon turned them east, towards the Painted Hills. The red soil of the path they were on made Cheyanne feel vaguely uneasy. It looked the color of dried blood. The grass on either side of them, what little there was, was as yellow and dry as barn straw.

The Painted Hills were still a long way off, the first of them barely visible on the horizon. But even as far off as they were, they could see the rusty red and chalky yellow striping on the distant butte that gave the place its name. Brainerd had been uneasy at first about being in the open on the flat plain, but swallowed his distaste when Doctor Lisbet raised an eyebrow and inquired, "How guilty is your conscience, for heaven's sake? Is there any direction from which you are *not* being hunted?"

"The direction we're going," Brainerd muttered. "Because anyone with sense knows to stay away from there."

Fallon hawked and spat. "I knew it'd be helpful to our morale havin' you along, Nels. We all feel better about our own selves seeing what a miserable cuss you still are after all these years."

Brainerd just grunted. Cheyanne was surprised at this—she had thought a remark like that would have provoked someone as irritable as Brainerd into a fight. She decided that, with his memories somewhat restored, the blond man must have remembered that Fallon was habitually acerbic with everyone.

She said as much to Doctor Lisbet, who smiled ruefully in response. "Jonas and Brainerd used to needle one another almost constantly. It may be a male ritual, because Jonas never teased any of us with as much venom as he did Larry and Nelson. I think we are all falling into our old habits, riding together like this," she added. "I still wish you had stayed behind but I cannot deny that it has been good for us to have you along."

"Really?" Cheyanne was pleased.

"She means we behave a little better for you, squirt." This was Fallon, who seemed to have almost preternatural hearing. He glanced back at the two women over his shoulder and grinned. "Even old Nels here seems to be reining in his worst impulses." He nodded forward at the blond man, who was riding at the head of their little procession. "Helps not to have any liquor along, of course."

"That's new for you, as well," Lisbet remarked dryly.

"Well, hell, once you get hooked on lavender donkey piss, it ruins you for whiskey." Fallon said it with a completely straight face but it made Doctor Lisbet and Cheyanne laugh out loud, and even Brainerd let out a stifled snort.

The man in black grinned at the two women, pleased with the effect his words had. "Good to see you ladies laugh a little."

"Women usually laugh at you, don't they, Jonas?" Brainerd clearly could not resist.

"Ayup." Fallon was unfazed. "But with me it's a'purpose. And only when I'm fully dressed, unlike *some* fellers of my acquaintance." Brainerd let out a low growl and Fallon added innocently, "…namin' no names of course."

"Please, gentlemen," Doctor Lisbet put in. "Can we not change the subject? Jonas, do you have any sense of the others? We seek Lawrence and Aaron still, yes?"

"Nothing yet," Fallon admitted. "Thought I'd caught a smell of Aaron yesterday but it was just for a minute or two and it's gone now. You?"

"I am not as facile as you." Doctor Lisbet frowned. "Which surprises me a little, I must admit. I recall you used to fear the Language."

"Still do." Fallon shrugged. "Quitting drinking helped though. Easier sorting Hermetics with a clear head. And… it makes the silver worse if I'm drinkin'. Found out the hard way my head for liquor's pretty much gone."

The silver was on all three of them now; both Brainerd and Lisbet's eyes were permanently silvered along with Fallon's, and when Cheyanne asked about the screaming Doctor Lisbet would only say that it was bearable for the moment. Other than a grimace, Brainerd did not comment at all.

This exchange served to dampen the conversation for a while. Cheyanne wondered if the others were remembering things about Stonegarden, and then she wondered if her thoughts were visible in her aura, whatever that looked like. It was eerie to think that Fallon and Lisbet could see what she was thinking just by looking at her. Eerie, and a little unnerving. She was trying to think of a tactful way to ask Doctor Lisbet if there was perhaps a way to make herself not quite so sparkly as Fallon had told her she was, when she heard a gunshot.

"Jonas, do you have any sense of the others?"

"What was that?" Lisbet's head came up sharply.

"Wagon and riders," Brainerd said. "Up ahead. Little draw up there between them two hills." He pointed. "Looks like some pilgrims have bought themselves some trouble. Road agents maybe."

"Veer off here," Fallon said. "We'll circle round the other side of the hill there, keep our distance."

"But aren't we going to help them?" Cheyanne could not help blurting it out. "We have to do something!"

"Not our business," Brainerd said. "We ain't marshals."

Cheyanne turned to Fallon and Lisbet. "He's not wrong," Doctor Lisbet said. "We don't know what's going on. We should not get embroiled in other people's troubles."

Fallon almost nodded in agreement, but Cheyanne could see his uncertainty. She pressed him. "Didn't you tell me that you quit the Confederate army because of things like this? Innocent people being attacked on the road for no reason?"

"That was different," Fallon said. He scowled at Cheyanne.

"Of course it is!" Cheyanne was getting angry. "Because now, you can do something about it! All three of you, you can do miraculous things! You have abilities that… that… what good are they if you don't use them to help people?" she finished, awkwardly.

For a moment no one said anything.

Finally Doctor Lisbet sighed. "The girl shames us all, Jonas." She smiled at Cheyanne. "All right. Let's go see what is happening. It might be perfectly innocent."

"Fool's errand," Brainerd said. "All right, then. You all can go on ahead if'n you want but I'll just head on around the rise there and see you on the other side of the draw. Jonas? You with me or the womenfolk?"

Fallon shook his head. "I don't like it but I'm not letting these two girls ride into a shooting matter without siding them." He snorted. "Should have known *you* would."

Brainerd glared at Fallon. "Always thinking the worst. You don't think it's best we come at them from two directions? No wonder you quit the Army, you are useless as a soldier. Here's how we do this. You go straight up with Lisbet and the girl, keep 'em talking while I circle round and come at 'em from the other side of that little hillock there. You ain't no use to me without a gun anyway. Least the doctor lady can shoot."

"I would prefer we handle this without any shooting." Lisbet took a deep breath. "The plan is sound, though. Let's go." Without waiting for an answer, she kicked her heel into Sultan's side and was off at a gallop. Fallon and Cheyanne wheeled their mounts and followed.

It was a small covered wagon, driven by a man and woman with a small boy sitting between them. In front of them were three men on horseback and a fourth holding the reins of his horse in one hand while in the other arm he cradled a shotgun aimed at the wagon. All of them turned to face the new arrivals.

Fallon slid off his horse and stepped forward. "What's this all about? We heard some shooting."

The man with the shotgun nodded at the three in the wagon. "Ain't it obvious? This is Oregon. They's pilgrims. These folks can't settle here. That's a hangin' offense."

Cheyanne blinked and felt a little sick. Suddenly it was clear.

Because the family in the wagon was black. Cheyanne knew that it was the law that no Negro was allowed to own property in Oregon. She had taunted Fallon with his desertion during the war and here the same situation was again: armed men threatening to murder a black family, and it was legal as could be. She glanced over at Fallon and saw from the grim set of his jaw that the parallel was not lost on him, either.

"You would shoot this family on the chance they *might* settle here?" The contempt in Doctor Lisbet's voice was a palpable thing. "What stout guardians of the law you are, to be sure. Are you deputized? On what authority do you do this?"

"It's the law," the man with the shotgun said, but he was less sure of himself now.

Fallon spat. "And the fact that they've got a wagonload of goods and you look like the ragged end of an empty feedbag don't got nothing to do with it. Robbery, dressed up nice and legal because who cares about dead darkies in Oregon? The lady's right, the courage you show is a fearsome thing." His drawl indicated it was anything but. "Maybe you could just ask 'em to move on and move on your own selves."

"Maybe we could just have you move on instead, mister." This was one of the men on horseback. "We got guns and this ain't your business anyhow."

"Making it my business."

Fallon was still speaking in an easy, conversational drawl, but Cheyanne saw his shoulders were tense, and she could feel the charge building between Fallon and Doctor Lisbet as she silently mouthed the Language.

Fallon said softly, "Lisbet? Don't you think he's seen enough?"

Lisbet nodded. *"You're blind,"* she said to the man with the shotgun. *"And you, and you."*

The words came out in the same strange, layered voice that Cheyanne had heard her use on the Barker brothers back in the Metolius country. Immediately, the man with the shotgun released his hold on his horse and clapped a hand to his eyes. The other two riders Lisbet pointed at did the same.

"What the hell?" one of them screeched. "Can't see! She did this! Eben! Make her stop it!"

The one remaining rider that could still see stared in terror at where Lisbet sat calmly astride her horse. "Yes, Eben, do," Lisbet said to him. "See if you can make me do anything. Perhaps we'll have something different for you. Maybe you would like to have all the blood explode from your heart. Or cancer. Or..."

"Stop playing with 'em, you two." Brainerd approached from the rear of the wagon, his gun drawn. He gestured at Eben and the other blinded road agents. "Fix 'em so they can see and send them on their way."

"How's that sound, Eben?" Fallon spread his hands. "You leave these nice folks be and ride on, no harm done... or we do something like this." He pointed and Eben screamed in such terrible pain that for a moment Cheyanne thought Fallon had killed him.

Fallon dropped his hand and the unfortunate Eben gasped and went limp, almost falling off his horse. "You... what *are* you?" he wheezed.

"Pissed off. In a hurry. Not someone to mess with." Fallon said. Abruptly his voice lost its pleasant, conversational tone. "Understand me, boy?"

Eben nodded. Lisbet fluttered a hand and the other riders suddenly blinked in surprise and relief, their sight restored. Fallon nodded at the man with the shotgun. "Move along, now."

The road agent looked at Fallon, then Lisbet, then Brainerd. "Your eyes... you ain't human."

"Maybe not, any more." Lisbet's voice sounded bleakly amused. "But we don't rob unarmed families, families with *children*, at gunpoint. We shall have to be satisfied with that."

"G'wan." Brainerd was out of patience. He waved his pistol at the man with the shotgun. "On your horse, now. Move."

Fallon added, "By the way. Next time you think of robbing a wagon, or anyone, y'all will start throwing up. Like this." He nodded at Eben and instantly the four riders all looked green. Fallon held up his right hand and then suddenly clenched it into a fist. At that, the riders all retched uncontrollably. One clutched his abdomen and fell off his horse.

It was almost comical, but Cheyanne did not feel like laughing.

Somehow seeing what Doctor Lisbet and the others were truly capable of frightened her, especially since she realized Brainerd was right. The road agents had never had a chance. Fallon and Lisbet had been playing with the robbers like a cat playing with a crippled bird. The man with the gun had said it: not human, and not just because of their eyes. The silver eyes of her companions looked terrifyingly unhuman, yes, but so did the expressions they wore.

"On your way, now," Doctor Lisbet said softly.

The four men did not dare to argue but simply rode away at a brisk trot. Cheyanne let out the breath she had been holding.

Fallon looked at Brainerd, nodded, then grinned at Lisbet. "See? No shooting."

Lisbet rubbed her forehead. "I almost think shooting would have been preferable," she muttered. "Dear lord, my head felt like it might burst there for a second."

Only then did they remember the black family still sitting silently, wide-eyed, in the wagon. Fallon turned to face them and tipped his hat. "You folks probably shouldn't linger," he said. "There might be other civic-minded Oregonians about."

The man swallowed. "You're them," he said, finally.

"Huh?" Brainerd blinked. "We're who now?"

"The silver riders," the woman said. "Aaron said you were coming. He saw it in dreams. But we thought..."

"Aaron?" This was Lisbet, her voice sharp and severe. "Aaron is with you?"

"At the settlement," the man said. "He... he guards us. From men like those."

Fallon looked closely at them. "Aaron's with you? He has silver eyes too? Like us?" He took off his dark spectacles to reveal his own gleaming silver irises. "Take us to him."

The man hesitated. Cheyanne added, "Please. We mean no harm. We're friends. Honest." She turned to the others and added, "Tell them."

Doctor Lisbet nodded. "The girl speaks true. Aaron is our friend. But we need to speak to him."

The man looked at the woman. She nodded and turned to face Lisbet. "Follow us, then." The woman in the wagon smiled briefly. "In fact we invite you to stay with us. I'm Coretta Jones. My husband's Denny and this little one is Eli. We thank you kindly for what you did."

The boy, Eli, leaned forward, his eyes wide. "Are you regular people?" he asked. "Why are your eyes like that?"

Coretta shushed him but Fallon just laughed. "Boy, when you figger it out, you tell me and we'll both know. Let's go see Aaron, now."

• • •

The wagon led their little procession to a creek that ran towards a small valley with jagged cliffs rising on either side. Eventually they reached a small settlement made of mostly tents and teepees, though there were a few wooden shacks here and there.

"You live here?" Fallon asked Jones. "Hell of a risk, ain't it? I don't care m'self but the law's pretty clear about Nigras owning property in these parts."

The man in the wagon nodded. "I expect so. But we wouldn't be able to travel without getting stopped anyways, even if we showed we was on our way to Idaho or Washington territory. You saw." He shrugged. "We don't really own the property, anyhow, ain't like we staked any claim or anything like that. Technically we's just camping. Out here in this desert country, not on any roads, hardly anybody comes across our little valley. Ain't no white folks filed on it because no one knows it's here. We live quiet. Couple other black folks and us, a few Injuns. All folks got chased out of they own homes for one reason or 'nother."

"A communal sanctuary of sorts, then." Doctor Lisbet sounded intrigued at the simplicity of it. "And you manage without any outside contact at all? Are you vegetarian? Grow your own food? I would not think the land could sustain a settlement, even a small one like this. Yet you appear to be in good health."

"They's fish in the creek, we got a few potatoes and such. We get by." Coretta smiled wanly. "But as it happens that's how we ran into that trouble. We took a chance on traveling to the trading post by Randall to pick up a little flour and seed corn for our group. Those men must have followed us back from there." She sighed. "Had to take the chance, though, winter's coming. And if we'd sent one of the Indian families they'd have had worse." She brightened. "But now you are here. It's because of such happenings that I have to believe the good Lord has a plan."

Cheyanne saw Lisbet wince a little. The doctor had never been much on divine plans, or even religion. Fallon snorted and said, "Well, someone's plan, anyway. Can't deny it feels like we been led a lot of the time lately."

Brainerd looked around the little camp. "Where's Aaron at?"

Denny Jones pointed. "His tent is yonder. He looks after his friend. The red one."

Lisbet raised an eyebrow at this, but Fallon only shook his head. They dismounted and walked slowly towards the tent Jones had indicated, and Cheyanne and Brainerd did likewise.

Fallon leaned in through the flap. "Aaron? It's me and Lisbet and Nels. You in there?"

"I am here, Jonas." Cheyanne thought the voice was one of the richest and deepest she had ever heard, though also one of the softest and saddest. "I'm glad you've finally come, though I'm afraid I bring you only grief."

They pushed their way into the tent. It was lit by one small kerosene lantern, though after a moment Cheyanne realized that it could not possibly be kerosene; the smell was all wrong. It was something sweet and yet acrid, something like sage or juniper, perhaps. The man hunkered down over the cot was a black man of indeterminate age; he could have been anywhere between thirty and sixty. He looked up at them and smiled briefly. She realized that the silver had overtaken him more than any of the others; not just his eyes and hair, but even his dark skin had a metallic sheen. "Jonas. And Lisbet of course. Nels I know as well. But this one I don't know."

"I'm Cheyanne." She tried to keep her voice from squeaking. "I'm..." She paused, unsure of how to explain.

"You're Lisbet's." Aaron squinted at her a moment. "A foundling. But not. Not really. You're here a'purpose, same's the others, even if the silver's not on you." He smiled gently. "You are welcome here, missy, in any case."

He's reading my sparkly aura, Cheyanne thought. *I guess everybody can. I might as well just get used to it.*

"Who's this feller?" Fallon moved forward. "That the red one they..." His words trailed off. He stared at the figure on the cot. "Jesus wept, Aaron. Is that *Larry*?"

The man on the cot made no sign. He might have been catatonic. Cheyanne could see him, now. He was stripped to the waist, one threadbare blanket covering him. His skin was red and leathery, almost reptilian. His eyes, open and unseeing, were flooded with silver; not just the iris, as Fallon's and the others were, but all that was visible of them, as though the entire socket had been filled with molten metal. Were it not for the nearly imperceptible rise and fall of his chest he might have been dead.

"It's Larry. What's left of him." Aaron's sonorous tone held no bitterness, just grief and fatigue. "He fell to the obsidian. We's all going to end up this way if we don't stop it."

"No riddles, Aaron." Doctor Lisbet's voice was sharp and hard. "None of this makes any sense. What do you know of the obsidian? You were the cook, you never troubled to learn the Language. Why is this happening now? What is your role in all of this?" Her voice was trembling just a tiny bit and Cheyanne realized how deeply frightened she was. This frightened Cheyanne herself, more than anything else had up to that point.

Aaron turned and faced all of them. His expression was calm, but in his way he looked as fearful as Lisbet. Not like for his life, but more the look of a man who must make a terrible choice, Cheyanne thought suddenly. Afraid for his soul.

"I know y'all are scared," Aaron said. "I understand that. I hear her screaming in the silver, the same as you do. I can't explain it all. But I know that Anne-Marie is not dead, and I fear that Ezekiel is not dead yet either. But even if he himself is gone, he's awakened something dark and terrible."

"Like what?" This was Brainerd, an edge in his voice. "What did this to Larry?"

He's shook too, Cheyanne thought.

Aaron shook his head. "Don't know. Not exactly. But it's coming. And we's the only folks that can stop it. The Kuyagah are gone now, 'ceptin the couple old ones we got here in the camp. And mebbe the little one, there." He nodded at Cheyanne, who could only stare in shock. "But we're the ones trained, we got the Language. It has to be us."

"You too?" Doctor Lisbet was not satisfied. "But who trained you?"

"Who d'you think?" Fallon looked sourly amused all of a sudden. "Wasn't that eastern snob Zeke, for all his highfalutin' talk about building a new society. No way he'd teach Language to a Nigra. And you never sat in with any of us. Anne-Marie did it. Behind our backs. That about right, Aaron?"

Aaron nodded. "She taught me just to read and write, first. The Language just sorta followed. There's a lot you don't know. Me either, but I can tell you what I can. But let's get you all round some food first," he added with a sudden smile, one with real warmth in it this time. "Y'all can judge if I still got my old cookin skills."

He stood and they followed him out. Cheyanne heard Lisbet mutter, "The condemned ate a hearty meal."

● ● ●

Eight

The Slave & the Lover (Aaron's Story)

Supper was a communal open-air affair, loosely hosted by the Jones family in front of their adobe-and-sod shack, with Aaron serving as chef. He was grilling corn on the cob and various cuts of meat on an iron grill over a firepit made of rocks, humming snatches of song as he turned the meat and joked with Eli and the other children that hovered nearby. He was clearly a favorite, and no one seemed bothered by his eerie silver eyes or his metallic skin tone. Near to where Aaron was barbecuing, there were a few rudely built tables and benches on a patch of grass that served to form the informal center of the community. Here it was that Fallon, Lisbet, Cheyanne and Brainerd sat and watched Aaron and his people, as the supper gathering slowly coalesced around them. Coretta Jones emerged with plates of biscuits to put on the table. At Lisbet's raised eyebrow, Cheyanne rose to help her, and Coretta beckoned her to follow into the shack.

"It's so pretty here," Cheyanne told her. The cliffs that surrounded the camp were chalky orange and red, but down here in the little valley between them where the creek ran, it was green and almost lush, though the trees were still sparse and spindly. "I can see why you stay."

Coretta's answering smile was weary and a little sad. "We ain't got much choice," she said. "Once we move we'd have to keep moving, and on back roads, probably, till we got to California. They's only about seven of us colored folks here, us and Levi's family what we came west with, but that's still more'n is legal to settle in Oregon. Idaho or Washington territory ain't much better. We can't make a long trip like that now, with winter coming. Not with the little ones." She nodded at where Eli and the other children were playing in the grass.

"How did you end up here anyway?" Cheyanne blurted. "I mean—I don't think the law is right, I think you should be welcome no matter what your color is. Doctor Lisbet says there's not any medical difference between races at all, not Indian or Chinese or anybody, everyone is just human. But if you knew about Oregon—"

"We didn't know." Coretta's expression darkened. "None of us can read, except Aaron, and he wasn't with us then. Folks are just s'posed to know, I guess. None of our family or friends hadn't ever made it out this far, we didn't talk to no one who mighta warned us off. All we knew was that nothing west of the mountains wasn't ever no slave state. That's all we wanted. Even after the War and Mr. Lincoln made his proclamation that we was all free, the South was no place for us, not with them Texas vigilantes burning out black families whenever the mood struck them. So Denny and me, and Levi and his family there—" she pointed. "Well, we loaded up our wagons and took off. We figgered on starting fresh. We weren't coming to Oregon anyways. We were trying for north California, we come west from Texas through Nevada. We'd heard tell of the forest country by the coast and Denny knows his way around woodworking and logging and such. We thought he could hire on at a camp and we'd find a nice place of our own, build a cabin and plant a garden, live quiet… but we had some ill luck." She waved a vague hand toward the east. "We didn't figure on the trip being so hard, or that the mining towns would be so rough. I mean, there was no place for us in Texas, but out here weren't much better. The government passed those Enforcement Acts against the Klan and such but there wasn't much enforcement. Still plenty of vigilante riders hanging black folks, burning their homes. We knew if we were going to raise our boys and live safe we had to get out, and north and west was the best way. We thought the free states would be more welcoming. We found out they wasn't."

Listening to Coretta's matter-of-fact recital, Cheyanne felt vaguely ashamed. She was a half-breed herself, but no one had ever treated her as anything other than white. If anything, she was privileged, because in Hackett Creek she was regarded as the daughter of Doctor Lisbet and the community's respect for the doctor elevated her own status a little. She couldn't think of anything to say to Coretta that would not sound inane, or worse, condescending. So she remained silent.

Coretta sighed. "Couple times road agents tried to hold us up and no law seemed to care. We stood 'em off but we knew how it would go if'n a Negro shot a white man, even if the white man was a robber. It was just a matter of time afore someone like that forced Denny to shoot to kill. So Denny and Levi put they heads together and decided we'd go away from roads and people, take our chances with Injuns in wild country."

There was an awkward pause. "I'm sorry," Cheyanne said, finally. "People can be awful."

"Some are," Coretta agreed. "So we took to moving cross-country and we just plain got lost trying to find our way west. Mountains east of here, the weather's so bad you can't see the sky half the time and not much sun. And then our youngest, Eli's brother, took sick and we lost him coming over the mountains last winter." Her voice caught a little. "We was scared to stop then, since by then we sorta had figgered we wasn't supposed to be here. We probably should have waited out the winter somewhere holed up like the bears do. But we ran and somehow, coming out of the mountains into the desert, we got all turned around. I don't even know exactly where my baby boy is buried," she added, sadly. "Anyway, this is where we landed. Seemed safe enough and these Injun folks here made us welcome. We thought we'd finish out the winter here and move on last spring. But when Levi went up to the post at Randall they almost killed him. More riders. That's when we found out about the law in Oregon. He got away, but then we was all terrified. These Injuns, they're farmers, not fighters. Law don't protect them any more than us. I thought we was done, to be honest." She smiled. "But then Aaron came. He done something to the valley here, I don't know what, but folks meaning us harm… they can't find their way in, even if they're riding with us." She nodded at Cheyanne. "That's how we know you and your people are safe, honey. Aaron's protections would have stopped you at the cliff otherwise."

"He used the Language." Cheyanne understood now. "This really is a sanctuary then."

"He helps us all. The Indians say he is a shaman of the earth, that's why he looks like he's got metal in his eyes. Your folks must be the same, I don't know about that. But Aaron's a good man, and educated. He even said he was thinking on starting a little school for us in the evenings, but then the red man come. Poor Aaron's been at his side day and night, trying to save him." Coretta shrugged. "My daddy would have said that red feller coming to Aaron proved his doings was devil's work but I seen the devil in men and it ain't Aaron, or even that poor sick man with the red lizard skin. It's them fellas in white hoods chased us out of our home, or those bandits your friends scared off. The devil in men's hearts is the one to be wary of, especially the one that claims righteousness for his doings. Our lord Jesus said that in the Bible, I think." She looked wistful. "If I had my letters I could read it for m'self. Levi has an old family Bible from his pa but he can't hardly read it none. Someday, maybe."

"I don't know," Cheyanne admitted. "Doctor Lisbet's not much on church. But I have heard her say much the same about evil and men's hearts."

Coretta patted her shoulder. "Well, church or no, she raised you right, I think. Come on and help me set the table 'fore them hungry menfolk start raising a ruckus."

Cheyanne giggled. Coretta handed her an armload of plates, then picked up another basket of rolls herself, and the two went back out to the tables.

• • •

Later, after Cheyanne and Coretta had cleared the table and sent the children down to the creek to fetch water to wash the plates, the gathering slowly broke up. Soon it was just the few from Stonegarden, Cheyanne, and Denny and Coretta Jones sitting around the firepit as the coals burned low. Cheyanne looked up at the stars and thought, *this really is a sanctuary, a place of rest.* Even with Lawrence, or whatever Lawrence had become, in the tent a few yards away as a reminder of the mission they were on, everyone around her looked at peace.

"Well, that was certainly a fine meal, Aaron," Doctor Lisbet said, and smiled. "You haven't lost your touch. The chicken salad was really quite something."

Aaron grinned. "Wasn't chicken," he said. "That was snake meat, spiced with a little juniper. Some taters mixed in. Good eatin.'"

Cheyanne gulped and Fallon looked a little nonplussed, but Lisbet just laughed. "Well, we are in the high desert country. One must make do. The steak, though, that was no reptile, surely."

Denny put in, "Naw, that was the last of a big ol' pronghorn buck the boys brought in a couple days back. Jacky and Eli went on their first hunt with Gray Cloud and some of the other young'uns from the tribe. They did real good."

Brainerd made a derisive noise. "We gonna get to it, Aaron, or are you and the doctor lady just going to exchange recipes?"

"There is such a thing as common civility." Lisbet glared at him. "I would think even a boor like you could thank our hosts for the meal. We are guests here."

Brainerd hawked, spat, and uttered an obscenity. Lisbet tensed a little and Cheyanne thought for a moment that she might do something awful to him, as she had done to the robbers earlier.

But Aaron merely sighed. "Naw, pull in your claws, Lisbet, he ain't wrong. We got dark business ahead of us and it don't get easier with waiting."

"We gonna get to it, Aaron?"

"Start with how you learned the Language, maybe," Fallon said. "And what happened to Larry."

Aaron shook his head. "I ain't sure of that second one. I can't quite feel his presence here at all; that is, the man we knew as Larry. I been trying to reach him with little result. Not sure he's even there in that red husk of a body, though the body itself lives. But I'll tell you what I know. Nels won't like it much, though."

"You the one took my memories?" Brainerd bristled at that. "Because if you done it... I'll—"

Aaron held up a hand. "No. it was Anne-Marie. And she done it to save my life. But I better tell it in order."

"Shut up, Nels," Fallon put in. "Let the man talk. Save your grudges for later."

Brainerd still looked flushed and angry, but he let it go. The others were silent as well, waiting.

Aaron said softly, "You have to understand, I wasn't like the rest of you. I wasn't called, they weren't no ravens or trickery like that, Ezekiel and Anne-Marie just found me. It was pure happenstance..."

• • •

He had been drifting a while, now. When the war had ended Aaron had thought he might try farming, but his heart wasn't in it, and the sheer novelty of being free to go anywhere he pleased was intoxicating. When he started west from Carolina he just kind of kept going for the next year or so, stopping here or there for a week to work odd jobs, till he ended up in north California. Did okay there for a while—he'd always been a good cook and he found out that miners, especially, liked to eat out on payday almost as much as they liked to drink. Generally in most of these boom towns there was some feller that was running a restaurant or a saloon that needed a cook, and Aaron learned how to negotiate a fair wage without ever losing the yessir-nossir humility that white folks seemed to require of him.

He could have just picked one of those places and settled but the wanderlust always got him. He took it in his head to see the mountains when he was in desert country, and when he was in the mountains he wondered about the plains. Always wanting to see what was next.

This endless curiosity was what had led to his current trouble. The girl and the bearded man had stopped in the saloon in Canyon City where

Aaron happened to be working that week, and their conversation had pricked his interest as he was grilling their meal (it was a concoction of his own, a savory mixture of eggs and potatoes and chicken and herbs that was never the same way twice, but had made the saloon hugely popular.) The hell of it was, he hadn't even been looking at the girl; he was curious about the bearded feller she was with, the professor. The blonde girl was surely a beauty but he had just been wondering about what the bearded man had been saying. Something about Indian tribes, and healing, and obsidian.

Eventually the bearded man left and the girl said something about being along in a while, but she lingered at the bar laughing and joking with the miners that vied for her attention. So she wasn't *with* the bearded man, not in that way, anyhow. The girl seemed to be enjoying all the attention, but deftly deflected any one of the men that sought to become a particular favorite. Aaron knew better than to watch but he listened with increasing amusement as he gathered up the dirty dishes and took them to the back. Somehow she was keeping them all at arm's length while creating the illusion of growing intimacy and friendliness with each one. She was such a tiny little thing. He hoped that none of the increasingly drunken miners would get tired of her games and just grab her.

Eventually she departed and, deprived of the floor show, most of the miners left as well. The rest of the evening passed quietly enough, but after closing, when Aaron finished his sweeping and locked up the saloon for the night he saw two of the drunken miners waiting for him.

"We seen you looking at that girl, boy," one of them said. "You need a lesson."

It wasn't true but that didn't matter. Aaron knew nothing would satisfy these men but violence—at best it would be a beating and at worst it would be his life. So he didn't wait. He shoved one of them into the other and took off running.

They were drunk and he was not, and he outdistanced them quickly, but he knew he had only minutes at most. No time to do anything but swing through the stable where he had been bedding down, grab his bag, and light out. He didn't dare stay in town, not even to collect his pay. Aaron knew the story the miners would tell and their drunken assessment of his intentions would be enough to hang him. Especially after he had dared to lay hands on them. Pleading self-defense was not an option when it was a black man's word against two white ones. So he ran.

Once he was well away from town and into the woods, Aaron relaxed a little, and even got to feeling philosophical about it. He was only out a couple of days' pay, really. He had been thinking about moving on soon anyway. Maybe it was fate.

He topped a small ridge and saw a wagon parked in a clearing with a campfire. The fire was still going, though it was close on to two in the morning. As he drew closer he saw that it was the girl and the old man.

"Hello the camp," Aaron said. He could not have said what prompted him to take the chance. Curiosity again, he supposed. And the girl had a kind face.

They both spun to face him, startled. Aaron held up his hands. "No trouble," he said, gently. "I've been walking a while and wondered if I might set a spell and share your fire."

"Late to be traveling." The older man paused and squinted. "You look familiar, son. Were you in the town we stopped in earlier?"

"At the saloon," Aaron admitted. "I was working there until... well, I guess it was time to move on."

"Oh? Folks coming after you?"

"Not yet." Aaron paused. "There was a difference of opinion about my conduct. I didn't want to make a fight of it. Not worth it."

The girl sat up, interested. "Really? But you looked so happy, making that wonderful dinner and doing the other kitchen things. I thought, how fortunate that man is to know his skills and be able to use them to good benefit."

"Hush up, Anne-Marie." The old man was still scowling at Aaron. "Boy, are you in trouble? Seriously now. Will there be law coming for you?"

"Shouldn't be." Aaron couldn't help adding, "Doesn't mean there won't be. No telling. I was being threatened. It was two against one, but they was white. And they probably got friends in town. I'm just driftin."

The older man nodded, accepting it. "You fed us well earlier; I think we at least owe you a meal. We don't have much, but—"

Aaron shook his head. "Thank you kindly, but I don't need to eat. Though I would take it as a great favor if you could let me rest here a while. I'll move on in the morning."

The girl—Anne-Marie? Was that what the bearded man had called her?—laughed. "It's almost morning now. Which way are you headed? You should travel with us. Ezekiel, don't be an old poop about it. This man can cook. That meal in town was the best we've had in a month and we have a ways to travel yet. Your cooking is frankly awful and Lord knows I have no domestic skills whatsoever. And he'll be company." She turned to

Aaron and smiled. "You are drifting, you say? Drift with us."

After a moment, the older man nodded. "Anne-Marie is impulsive, but she makes sense," he said. "There's hard country ahead of us. Three is safer than two."

Aaron nodded. "Fair enough. I'm obliged to you folks. I'm Aaron."

"I'm Anne-Marie." The girl smiled. "And the old grump is Ezekiel."

Aaron shook hands with both of them. He asked, "Hard country, you said? Where?"

"In the high desert," Ezekiel replied. "We are searching for a place not many know of. An Indian relic, the Obsidian Temple." He brightened. "You are a man who has traveled. Have you heard tell of it?"

"Afraid not." Aaron shook his head. "What's this place to you folks?"

"Knowledge," Ezekiel said. He smiled. "And perhaps much more. We shall see."

• • •

"That was how it started." The fire had burned low, giving Aaron's silver eyes and metallic skin a rust-colored shine. "Zeke talked like we was going to be searching but he led us pretty much right to it. I ain't sure but I think he might have had a little of the Language before we ever got to Stonegarden. I think the obsidian called to him, and he and Anne-Marie called the rest of you."

Fallon nodded. Lisbet said, "And you, Aaron? Were you called as well? You seem more affected by the silver than anyone else. Do you know why? What does it mean?"

"I only have guesses," Aaron said. "I do know that it's Anne-Marie reaching out to us. She's still alive somehow. I can hear her. Can't you?"

The others nodded but Brainerd leaned forward. "I still want to hear why you messed with my memory, boy."

The blond man's voice was edgy and threatening, but Aaron just smiled. "Anne-Marie took your memory to protect me. You would have killed me."

Brainerd looked baffled, but suddenly Fallon let out a short bark of laughter. "Damn, boy. Nels here, and Philip, and who knows how many miners and cowboys makin' a try… and by God, it's this Nigra cook what rang the bell. Ezekiel was so damn worried about Anne-Marie getting involved with one of us and she was already involved with you. All along. Yeah?"

"Not all along. Not at first." Aaron's voice was soft and sad, despite his rueful smile. "At first... we were friends. I'd never had a true friend before, and neither had she, really. You remember how Ezekiel Reardon was. Cordial and smiling but never friendly, not really. There was always calculation. But Anne-Marie was guileless. Well, no, that isn't the word, not exactly. She could be sly. But still innocent. You remember."

Cheyanne looked over at Brainerd to see how he was taking it. She had thought he would be angry. Instead, he looked thunderstruck. "*You*? You and her?" he blurted. "How in the—"

"The usual way, I imagine," Lisbet said tartly. "Let him speak, Nels. It was a long time ago. Your wounded pride is not important right now."

Fallon leaned forward. "Did Ezekiel know?"

"Anne-Marie was terrified he might find out," Aaron said. "Even when there was nothing to be found out she always was very careful about our time together. For the longest time we just were talking, is all, but she was still touchy about us being seen. She was teaching me to read, and then to read the Language. Mornings, mostly. While you all were studyin' and Zeke was in the temple with the obsidian. I taught her some cooking, too. We just liked to spend time together more'n anything. I hardly realized myself how I was fallin for her, nor she for me—" He stopped. "I'm sorry, I've never talked about this with nobody. But it wasn't anything we planned or nothing. It kinda sneaked up on both of us. I don't know, we weren't really thinking ahead on it. I knew there was no way I'd ever be able to get her to leave with me, and we was happy enough how it was. It wasn't like we could get married or anything like that if'n we left Stonegarden. And then... well... that one night right towards the end. Something had happened earlier with all of you. Some sorta argument or something. She came up to my cabin and she was crying..."

"That was when she did her mischief with the wine," Fallon said. "So that's where she ran off to."

Aaron nodded. "Yes. She told me she loved me but she was still afraid. I could tell she thought we were in danger."

Fallon blinked. "From Nels here? He talks tough, but—"

Aaron shook his head. "No. From Ezekiel."

• • •

Aaron was startled out of sleep by the scratching on the door of his cabin. He rose from his cot, not bothering to don anything over the longjohns he was wearing. He opened the door, unsure of what he would find, and suddenly found himself with an armful of Anne-Marie. "Oh God, Aaron, I've made an awful mess of everything. Please, let me in. I just want you to hold me for a while."

Slowly he guided her into the cabin as she clung to him. They sat on the cot together and he reached for the lamp, but she put a hand on his arm. "No. no light. Oh, Aaron, I'm such a fool. I couldn't bear the look in your eyes if I tell you what I have done." She fell against him and began to sob.

Aaron's mind was a whirl. He had not dared to admit to himself that for months now, he desperately had wanted to have this woman in his arms... but not like this. This was all wrong. He gently pried her away and looked at her, the moonlight streaming in from the cabin's window painting them both in shades of blue. "You gotta tell me, honey. What's wrong? How can I help?"

"You were already helping, until you pushed me away," she said softly. Her eyes swam with tears. "Don't you want me? I know you do. I can see it. I want you too." She paused. "It can't be wrong if it's love. Isn't that true?"

He looked at her, more confused than ever. His body was raging at him to gather her in but he held himself tightly in check, feeling unaccountably angry at her suddenly forcing the issue. His voice was hoarse with conflicting emotion. "Be careful what you ask me." He paused. "I ain't what you call worldly," he added. "I ain't never—"

"I haven't either." Her voice was almost a whisper.

"Really?" Aaron was so shocked that he didn't realize how it sounded at first. "I mean... but you're so bold with men," he finished, lamely.

"It's mostly for show. I have wanted you, always." She sighed a little. "But I knew it would enrage Ezekiel. He wants me to be pure; and I do love him. I could not bear his anger but... I need this, Aaron. I am so deathly afraid of dying unloved by a man. For a time I thought it might be Nels... but I can't. He is... too hard. You are so gentle and kind... I want it to be you. I want you. I love you."

It was what Aaron had dreamed of for months, but still he hesitated. "Even here... there's going to be trouble over a black man and a white woman."

Inexplicably, she thought this hilarious. "Oh, my dear sweet man, of course there is trouble coming. There is trouble coming for all of us. The obsidian... never mind all that. Just be with me. Hold me. Love me."

"I do love you. That's no lie." He realized it was true even as he said it. No more talk of mere friendship, nothing like that. He loved her and wanted her and would have given his life for her. It was just a fact. No point tiptoeing around it any more. Nevertheless, he asked, "Are you sure this is what you want?"

"I can't lie," she said simply. "None of us can until the morning. No one but you. Are you lying?"

"Never to you," he said, and took her in his arms.

• • •

The following morning there was no outward sign of what had happened the night before, not from anyone. Aaron and Anne-Marie had slept very little; she had crept out just before dawn, kissing him with regret. "I must not be seen. But I'm so glad it was you. You will never know how much."

He tossed and turned for another two hours, too exhilarated to sleep, and finally rose at seven to prepare the morning meal for the compound.

He had no real schedule once the meal was completed, other than tidying up and seeing to the dishes. Usually this was when Anne-Marie came to him for lessons but today she merely whispered to him, "Tonight," and that was enough. Aaron cleaned up his pots and pans and went back to his cabin, stretching out on his cot. He was thinking about a nap when he overheard conversation outside the cabin.

"Jonas." It was Lisbet's voice. "A moment. Would you look at this?"

"Sure. Whatcha got there, doc?" Fallon's voice, as usual, was lazy and good-humored, but Aaron heard it sharpen a second later. "Wait. What's this? I ain't as good at this as you'n Larry but that word looks like 'warning.' Or maybe 'forbidden.' What the hell is this?"

"You said it yourself." Lisbet's voice sounded clipped and pragmatic, as it usually did, but there was an undercurrent of fear in it that was new. "Hell. Look here, and here."

Papers rustled. "You sure of this? I mean, we are just feeling our way through the translatin' of the Language—"

"I am not sure, no." Lisbet let out a long sigh. "But I already discussed it a little with Lawrence yesterday, after lunch. Today he is …preoccupied. You know why."

"Ayup. That was an ugly scene last night. No more of that jug wine for me, for sure." Fallon's chuckle sounded bitter. Aaron wondered what had happened. It had apparently been traumatic for others besides Anne-Marie. "How you feeling, Lisbet?"

"I have a roaring headache, and I am somewhat embarrassed. But this is more important." A pause. "Jonas… I only found this by looking at the stones myself. Ezekiel has withheld these passages from us. We were given the instructions but not the accompanying warning, not the *purpose*. This place… it is not a temple. It is a prison."

Fallon's drawl held bleak humor. "For us, or for the thing described in these papers?"

"Be serious." Lisbet's tone sharpened. "Jonas, I think Ezekiel means to free this thing. I think that is why we are here. We are all complicit."

"Lisbet. Are you really sure of this? Ezekiel… welp. I can't deny he's a little off, like one of them fire 'n brimstone revival types, maybe. He's driven. But what you are talking about… I can't see it. I mean, what would be his reason?"

"Power. Like a god." Pause. "Or a demon."

"Issat what this word is?" Paper rustled. "This is just jabber. Azathoth? Shabbat-Ka? I don't know what the hell that is."

"I don't either. I am using my best phonetic approximation based on the work we have done. But look here, and here. 'One must never restore the obsidian.' Restore, re-weave, reconstruct… something. I'm not sure. But Ezekiel's in there *all the time* now, Jonas. Sometimes he stands knee-deep in those black chips… just standing, silently, staring at the runes. I tiptoe so as not to disturb him, on the assumption that he is cogitating upon their meaning. But what if he is… listening? To something… I don't know. Something alien."

"Well, what if he is? This is all pretty alien, Elizabeth. And after last night I don't think any of us can lay claim to bein' all there. You're talking like the old man's talking to devils and such. He's our friend, Lisbet. He saved your life."

"Perhaps he has been seduced," Lisbet said after another pause. "We could… stop it somehow. Make him stop."

"Confront Ezekiel? Be serious. His power's more than all the rest of us together could handle, even if we had Anne-Marie on our side. And I ain't sure she would be. She loves that old man, and she loves the power. You've seen it."

A pause.

Lisbet's voice. "We could just go, then. Nothing holds us here."

"True enough." Fallon's voice was thoughtful. "That what you want? Just leave the others?"

"Nels can look after himself. We should warn the rest, though. Larry and Theo and Aaron. Quietly. If these words mean what I think they do, then… whatever Ezekiel plans, it cannot end well. We have been ill used,

I think. Our skills and scholarship… in our need to escape the world outside, I believe we have been recruited into something dark and terrible."

"All right." Fallon's voice sounded heavy and sad. "I'll talk to Nels. He's a bastard but I think he deserves better than to be made into an 'emissary' to… what is this again? The 'Hell's Gate'?"

"Gate, opening, mouth. Something." Lisbet's chuckle was humorless. "Something Ezekiel plans to open. I only hope that with us gone, he will be unable to do so."

"All right. I don't think he's close to being done yet, Lisbet, so us leaving should be enough. Let's head out tomorrow night. We'll take a day and talk it through with the others, on the sly. Try'n keep away from Zeke as much as you can. Even a lunkhead like me can see the worry floatin' around that aura of yours. It's sticking out like cactus needles."

"I doubt we will see much of him. He is isolating himself among the runestones. We have had no notes from him for the last two days."

"All the better for us then. Just keep your head down till it's time to go, Lisbet. Tomorrow we ride, you 'n' me 'n anyone else wants out. It'll be all right."

The voices faded and Aaron heard steps receding in the gravel. Was this why Anne-Marie had come to him at last? Out of fear? But no, it could not be. Maybe at first but even someone as inexperienced as he was with a woman could tell when he was being lied to, and her aura last night had sparkled with love and joy. It was a pure thing between them, he knew it.

But still… they must flee. He knew that too. When she came to him again that night, he would tell her. There was somewhere they could go to be together, Aaron was sure. Somewhere in the world where they could live and love in peace.

Somehow he got through the rest of the morning and even preparing the midday meal. Fortunately no one noticed how distracted he was. He could sense an awkwardness over the whole group.

Dinner was as awkward as lunch, though Aaron noticed Anne-Marie was making more of an effort to be antic and humorous than usual, as if to compensate for the sense of gloom that hung over the gathering. He caught her eye once or twice and somehow the smile she gave him in return seemed more affectionate than usual. He reveled in it. It was all going to work out.

Normally the evening meal would, as likely as not, slowly become a campfire gathering where the group would laugh and tell stories and occasionally drink to excess. But tonight no one seemed to be in the mood and Aaron was relieved to see most of the group disappear after supper was cleaned up.

In his cabin, he waited for Anne-Marie. He sat in darkness, as before. Shortly he heard a rustling at the door and she was there. Determined, Aaron said, "I have to…"

"Hush," she said. "No talk. Not now. Later."

Then she was in his arms again and his determination melted away. There was only the moment and the woman and the heat between them.

This time was better, less awkwardness, and no tears from her. She curled against him like a cat afterwards and Aaron almost fancied that she was purring. "I wish it could just be like this forever," she said.

"We could make it so," Aaron said. "Ain't no reason not to. We can't be married but we can be together. It's a big country. We'll find a place."

"But this is our place!" Anne-Marie sat up, shocked. "We can't leave!"

"Baby, there's evil here. Those black stones…"

"I can't go." Her shoulders shook. "You must not ask me."

Then the door flew open and Nels Brainerd stood there silhouetted against the moonlight. "I will be goddamned," he said. His voice was thick and harsh. "You and the nigger. Not me. The nigger *cook*." His hand flew to the pistol on his belt. "Well I am gonna fix that right—"

A golden glow erupted from Anne-Marie's hands. *"You never saw this, not any of it!"*

Her voice was layered and eerie. The glow wrapped itself around Brainerd, enveloping him. He froze in place.

"What—" Aaron swallowed. He stared at the nude girl next to him, whose hands still pulsed with yellow light. "What did you do?"

"I took his memories of me," Anne-Marie said. She let out a bitter laugh. "The ruination I have brought to him, at least, I can fix." She said to Brainerd, *"Leave this place. Ride on. Your life will be as it was if we had never met. Forget all of us."*

The glow faded from Brainerd. Silently he nodded, turned and strode away.

Aaron got up and closed the door to the cabin. He stood and looked back into the darkness at the pale shape of the girl on the cot. "We should ride on too," he said. "Please. If you love me. Let's get dressed right now and go. Ezekiel—he is going to try and make us—I don't know. Emissaries. Something like that. I heard Lisbet talking about it. Hell's emissaries."

"It's not what you think." Anne-Marie's voice was shaky. "I have to… all right. We'll go. We've ruined it all anyway." She did not sound regretful.

Aaron took her in his arms and held her for a long moment. "We haven't ruined nothing," he said. "We found each other. I don't much believe in anything but I do believe we was meant for one another. You believe that too, don't you?"

"I know exactly what I was meant for," she said. "I've known for years. But I don't care. I want you. Yes, Aaron, I'll go with you. Just… get dressed. I'll put some clothes on and bring the horses round. Sultan will fuss if there's more people there." She was sliding into her gingham dress even as she was speaking. "But there's something I have to do first. Wait here for me."

"I should go with you." Suddenly Aaron was afraid. He knew somehow that she was lying to him, but he didn't understand why. "Where are you going? If it's dangerous—"

"I have to make sure we're free." And then she was gone.

• • •

"That was the last I saw of her," Aaron finished. "After about ten more minutes came the explosions and the fire. I ran outside, and saw the ground crack and the abbey building fall into it. The whole mountain was coming down and I couldn't find anyone. So I ran. I looked at the stables and I saw Sultan was already gone. I thought she rode off without me… and then I heard her dying scream." He paused. "In my head and heart, like. Not really hearing it. But I never stopped feeling it."

Fallon nodded. "We been hearing it too. Feeling it. Whatever."

"So what does it mean?" Brainerd's voice was gritty and harsh. "The whole thing's a joke. She never loved me. She never loved you either, likely, boy. And she 'n Zeke 'n everyone who ain't sitting here all fell into a big hole in the ground. It's over."

"It can't be over," Lisbet said softly. "Think. Putting together the pieces we have, it becomes apparent that if Anne-Marie did not die, Ezekiel must not have died either."

"So?" Brainerd spat. "Not our concern."

"But it is," Lisbet said. "He must have drafted new… emissaries. He still means to open this gateway. Only we can stop them."

"Yes."

It was a new voice, soft and tentative, coming from behind them. They all turned to see the red thing that was once Lawrence standing unsteadily at the edge of the firelight, wrapped in a flannel sheet.

"Must …hurry," it said. "Not long now."

The others stared at the leathery red figure in shock. Finally, Fallon said, "Larry? You in there, buddy?"

"Almost," the red man said slowly. His words came with difficulty. "I … should be… gone… but… she saved a little. He sent me to find you… but she… she is fighting him. She asks my aid… Enough …to ride with you."

"Ride where?" This was Lisbet. "Is Stonegarden restored, then?"

"…No." The red man's face was eerily empty of expression, like a big red carving, Cheyanne thought. Yet the silver filling the eye sockets glowed a fierce white in the firelight. He went on, "But the …obsidian will be. It is …reshaping itself. Under the cliff… There is a cave. She… he—obsidian owns them both. We must… stop this. It is what… she asks of us."

Fallon nodded. He glanced at Aaron and Brainerd. "There it is, gents. Love ain't in it. We got a job to do."

Nine
Ravens & Wolves

They set out at dawn the following morning, not without some regret at leaving the comfort and serenity of the valley. Coretta insisted on packing their saddlebags full of dried meat and vegetables, and gifted Cheyanne with a rain poncho of marvelously soft cured deer hide as well. "Even here in the desert it still gets miserable cold and wet sometimes," she said. "You all are going into some hard country. Best be ready."

Cheyanne had stammered an awkward thanks and Coretta waved it off. "Aaron's family to us, and you folks are his family, so that makes us family as well. I don't know exactly what you all are riding into but I think it's going to be dangerous. Just be careful. And know you are always welcome here."

Cheyanne nodded, then impulsively leaned forward to gather Coretta in an embrace. "Thank you," she whispered. "We'll be back, I promise."

They set off in a small procession—Fallon in the lead, on his big bay Girl, then Brainerd on his rawboned Palouse, then Lisbet on Sultan and Cheyanne on Isobel, side by side, then finally Aaron on a sour-faced old mule that was roped to another mule carrying the red figure of almost-Larry bringing up the rear.

The red man seemed to float in and out of full consciousness. He would respond if asked a direct question, but he showed little volition of his own. Aaron had to walk him to the mule and help him to mount it, but then he would have just sat. Finally Aaron decided to just rope the animal to his own and lead them. This slowed the party to a walk but it was still better than going afoot.

They had been riding for some hours when Fallon called a halt. "Refill your canteens there." He pointed at a trickle of a creek to the left of the path they had been on. "Might be a little muddy but it's moving water, won't be too buggy nor stagnant. Not sure how much there'll be ahead of us. Let the horses drink too."

"How much further, do you think, Jonas?" Doctor Lisbet slid down off Sultan, then removed her hat and fanned herself with it. "I confess that I don't recognize this country at all."

"Day's ride. Maybe two, the way we're going. My thought was to come in from the north, avoid climbing the cliffs. I doubt that old trail survived the rockfalls and whatnot from that last night of the fire, we barely made it out ourselves then." Fallon nodded at the red figure sitting stolidly astride the mule. "Less our pal Larry's got a better notion. Where these caves of yourn at, anyhow?"

"The obsidian," the red man said. He raised a hand and pointed ahead of them, toward the cliffs in the east. "It pools in the earth, awaiting a sacrifice."

Brainerd snorted. "Well, ain't that helpful."

Lisbet made an impatient shushing noise. "Shut up, Nels. Lawrence—you are Lawrence still, yes? Can you not give us something more concrete? Some actual direction?"

The red man's brow knitted. His mouth struggled to form words.

Cheyanne said suddenly, "What does she tell you? Anne-Marie?"

"She is afraid," the red man said. "She... she hides her essence from him, but she knows he is growing stronger. Her hopes... lie within you. She asks you to be... avatars. Agents of the light."

Brainerd muttered an oath. Fallon and Lisbet both glared at him, but Cheyanne ignored it. She leaned forward, addressing the red man. "Then, if we are to bring the light? Who is the darkness? Who will we be facing?"

"Obsidian," the red man mumbled again. "The thing that lives in the rock."

"Is it Ezekiel, then, Lawrence?" This was Lisbet. "Did he survive somehow?"

"How much further do you think, Jonas?"

"Ezekiel. He is in the rocks, fallen into the pit. As I did, and Theo, and Philip. You will see. The obsidian craves sacrifice. It craves purity. It tries to take… it cannot work alone." The red man fell silent again, its lips working in a vague chewing motion. "It wanted Anne-Marie but… it was denied. Now it hungers again. We must… we must prevent its feeding."

"How?" This was Fallon, speaking sharply. "Goddammit Larry, give us something besides this mystery bullshit! You sound like some old witch woman. It's *us*, man, we're your friends, just talk to us for Christ's sake."

"Silver," the red man said, then stopped. The jaw worked silently for a moment. "The curse… of silver. You must bring the silver to him."

Abruptly, as though it were a marionette with the strings cut, the red thing slumped in the saddle and fell forward on to the mule's neck. It slid and would have fallen if Aaron had not quickly leaned over and braced it upright.

"Is he dead?" Lisbet asked.

Aaron shook his head. "Just gone asleep again. Coma or whatever. Like before. I don't know if'n that was Larry or some other talking through him. He ain't… I dunno, might be different for you all. But I can't see no aura off him at all. Like he's dead already. You see anything?"

Fallon and Lisbet both shook their heads no.

Brainerd rubbed his jaw and spat. "I don't know about you all," he said, "But I am starting to think this whole thing's a giant goddamn mistake. I'm tired of being played. First Anne-Marie, then you, and now this freak red thing. Hints and teases and nobody ever talking straight out. Gimme one good reason why we shouldn't part ways and ride off right now." He glared at the others and waited. "Well?"

There was an awkward silence.

Finally Doctor Lisbet sighed. "I know there is little use appealing to the better nature of a man who has never shown one, but consider the consequences of this, Nels. Can you really suggest that we just ignore this? Whatever he means by the obsidian, we know it is a deadly dangerous power, one that likely almost wiped the Kuyagah tribe off the face of the earth before they managed to imprison it… somehow. We can't just—"

"Hell we can't." Brainerd's brow narrowed with disgust. "I ain't no do-gooder and this is a fool's errand anyway. What've we got other'n your guesses and this red man's mysterious mumbles? We don't even know what we're riding into up there 'cept it's dangerous. Ever'body seems agreed on that, even if they can't say why."

Fallon scowled and spread his hands. "Fine. Ride on if you've a mind to.

God knows we're all sick of your bellyaching. Should have known you'd never stick it out."

He would have gone on but Aaron held up a hand. "Jonas. Don't start again. You two have fallen into your old bickering feud as though no years passed at all. Let's just skip to the end." He looked searchingly at Brainerd. "You know why you should ride with us. Because she asks it of you. You can hear Anne-Marie in the silver, same's the others here. Maybe you don't talk about it, maybe you try'n shut it out, but we can see it in your eyes. You hear her. And you can deny it all you want but I know you loved her. You are a hard man but she woke something in you once, something that made you better than you were."

Brainerd glared at him but did not deny it.

Cheyanne held her breath, waiting. Calmly, Aaron went on, "That's the man the silver is calling to. Maybe it really is her and we c'n save her. Maybe the silver's just an echo of her as she lay dying. But it ain't never gonna go away less we see this done. You always was a mean hardcase, Nels, but you ain't as mean as you think you are. She sent out her birds with a call for love, ten years ago, and you answered it."

"She was just playing me," Brainerd muttered.

"She was desperate," Aaron's voice was mild, his expression almost pitying. "She was scared of me and her. She was scared of Ezekiel. She was scared of what we was all turning into as we got better with the Language. Hell, I think she was scared of *herself*. She must have had some sense of what Zeke was planning. So she latched on to you as maybe being a way out, but she couldn't—" He spread his hands. "I don't know. I think maybe she didn't know her own mind, half the time. But I loved her. We all did. Even you. Sure, her ravens called you, but they didn't make you stay. You seriously going to try'n tell me you felt nothing for her? You gave up all your drinking and whoring and whatnot just to study old Injun rocks with a bunch of strangers? For months?"

As Aaron spoke, Brainerd's scowl had deepened, and now he exploded with an oath, adding, "Fine. Have it your way. You're all crazy and I'm the craziest one of all for going along. But the hell with it. Let's get this foolishness done." He spun and spurred the Palouse toward the distant hills without waiting for the others to follow.

After that they rode in silence. Even the horses seemed subdued.

The country was becoming much rougher now, mostly rocks and red clay with the occasional patch of dried-out grass the color of straw. Cheyanne noticed that they were climbing steadily higher as they went east. After another three hours' ride they were well into the foothills, surrounded by nothing more than orange and yellow cliffs. There was no living thing at all that they could see other than themselves... even the sparse grass was gone now. The path was largely gravel that was colored an unsettling blood-red. Cheyanne knew it was just clay but it still seemed ominous.

As the shadows lengthened, Fallon called a halt and turned to Aaron. "We ain't anywhere close to where we need to be and our water situation ain't great either. Stonegarden had a river at the bottom of the cliffs but these ain't them, and I think I misremembered the way somehow. I thought surely we'd have hit the northern fork of that river by now but I guessed wrong somewhere. We keep on this way we'll end up wandering in these rocks till we're nothing but bleached bone. I say let's make camp and then we go find water tomorrow."

Doctor Lisbet said, "Jonas, could Ezekiel have set a glamour to cloud our perceptions so we can't find the road to the abbey? Most all of us were led to the place by Anne-Marie's ravens. Perhaps it's not possible to get there without Hermetic guidance of some kind."

"Mayhap. But I don't think that's it." Fallon shrugged. "None of us have felt any kind of a tug or a whisper of anything like that, and we do have guidance, of a sort." He nodded at the red figure sitting slumped and silent on the mule roped to Aaron's. "Right now I'm more worried about water. We can manage on our canteens for another day or so, but the horses won't. If we don't find something soon we'll have to leave 'em to fend for themselves and go afoot."

Cheyanne's heart quailed at this. Leave Isobel and Sultan? The horses were almost as dear to her as Doctor Lisbet, and they were part of the family as far as she was concerned. But she knew Fallon was right. To keep on without water would certainly doom the horses, and possibly themselves as well.

There was silence for a moment. Finally Cheyanne said timidly, "Isn't there something you could do with Language? Find water that way?"

Fallon flashed her a rueful smile. "Don't work quite like that, sad to say, kitten."

"It's not magic," Lisbet added. "It is mostly a matter of altered seeing. Manipulating forces we already have all around us all the time. Auras and ley lines, the forces generated by the earth itself. With the aid of the Language we can shape and direct these forces somewhat, but we have no way to conjure into being something that is not there. Like a river, for instance." She sighed.

"Hell, I'd take a big puddle at this point." Fallon took off his hat, whacked it absently against his thigh, than donned it again. "I was hoping for, I dunno, some kinda spring or *cenote* or something, but I think the country's wrong for that. High desert like this ain't the same thing as, say, Arizona or Mexico."

Brainerd had gone ahead a little way and was now returning. He spat and said, "So now what? We ain't never getting anywhere if'n we have to keep calling a halt to palaver over everybody's damn feelings."

Fallon's eyebrows knitted and he would have no doubt produced a cutting remark but Aaron silenced him with a glance. He turned to Brainerd and said mildly, "We're trying to figure out how to water the horses so's we can push on tomorrow without killing 'em in this desert country. How much you know about these parts? Even a little trickle of a creek would do."

"Been thinking on that for the last hour or so," Brainerd admitted. "I know Hyacinth is somewhere to the south of us, half-day's ride maybe. Ain't much of a town; nought there other than a half-assed saloon and a stagecoach way station. But I remember the place was built close on to a little creek coming down from these same hills, made for a nice watering hole. S'why they put the station there. I was sure we'd run into that creek somewhere, I was scouting ahead tryin' to find it, but nothing I c'n see. I was thinking we must be too far north anyways. Nothing round here but red rocks and dirt. Don't none of you got a good idea of which way we're supposed to be going? None of this looks familiar to me but I thought it was just my screwed-up memory again. But if you all are just as lost as me—"

"I know we're *close*," Fallon snapped. "For Chrissakes, it was ten years gone and we all left going hell-for-leather in the middle of the night. Nobody was in the mood to be making any maps, so there's bound to be a little—"

"Gentlemen!" Doctor Lisbet's voice was the sharp crack of a whip, the tone that Cheyanne had heard her use when one of her patients was complaining too loudly. It worked here as well—the men fell silent and turned to look at her.

She pointed. "Apparently the old guides are still on watch."

They turned to see what she was pointing at. Four ravens perched on a boulder off to the side. The one furthest to the right cawed and lifted its wing, clearly indicating a cleft between the rocks. As they stared in wonder, the other three flapped into the air, then glided toward the cleft.

The one raven remaining hopped up and cawed again, then settled and extended the one wing once more.

"Nothing good will come of this," Brainerd muttered. "Damn birds."

"Got a better notion?" Fallon's drawl was sardonic as always, but with a note of resignation. "It's a direction, anyways. Might be water. Birds have to drink something. And that cleft's wide enough to take the horses. We was so stuck on climbing to the top o'these hills it never occurred to any of us to go between 'em."

The others hesitated.

Finally Brainerd muttered an oath and added, "What the hell, the whole thing's foolishness anyways. Come on, let's go." He wheeled the Palouse and the others followed, Aaron and the mules bringing up the rear.

After fifteen minutes or so of a slightly claustrophobic single-file procession between tumbled boulders, the cleft opened out into what appeared to be a dry canyon, a cut between cliffs made centuries ago by shifting plates of bedrock. Sheer walls of orange rock rose on either side of them, with the ground between layered over with thin and gritty sand. Ahead they could see an opening where the sky was turning purple with dusk, over the red and orange of the Painted Hills.

The ravens had lighted on a small shelf of rock ahead and to the left. They would go no further, but merely stood there, waiting.

"Now what?" Fallon sounded annoyed. "Trading one set of rocks for another don't seem like—"

"No, look!" Cheyanne pointed to the shadows under the rock shelf. "Water!"

It was indeed—a small natural spring, almost invisible under the granite shelf overhanging it. As they drew closer they could see that there was a pool that had formed at the bottom of the rocks.

Brainerd slid off his horse and led it to the pool, where it drank eagerly. "Welp. That's one for the damn birds after all, I guess."

The others followed suit. Aaron helped the red man off his mule and untied them, and both animals headed for the water without waiting to be led. In moments the horses and mules were lined up at the pool drinking thirstily, as orderly as though it was a stable trough. It would have almost been funny, Cheyanne thought, were it not for the somber errand that they were on. She glanced up, remembering the ravens, but they were gone. She turned to Lisbet. "The ravens – did Anne-Marie send them, do you think?"

Doctor Lisbet did not answer right away, but doffed her hat and fanned herself with it a little. Then she replaced it on her head and flashed Cheyanne a wan smile. "Honestly? I have no idea, little one." She sat on a boulder and sighed. "As events progress it seems things have become more mysterious, not less so." She nodded at Aaron and the red man that he was now gently leading to a resting place at the foot of the cliff opposite them, near the water. "That is not Lawrence, obviously, but the voice with which he speaks... the oracular pronouncements we heard earlier... he claims they are from Anne-Marie but I get no sense of her influence. In truth it makes me feel a little ill to look at him." Lisbet shook her head. "Lawrence was often prickly. But I was fond of him. We were friends. That—thing— it has his body, but it moves and speaks... I don't know, I suppose you would have had to know the man I knew back then to realize how alien that presence is to see now. Lawrence was *quick*. Quick of wit, quick of speech, quick of movement. That red thing moves and speaks as though it is barely conscious. I can't tell if there is anything left of our friend in there at all, though he claims it is so." She let out a quick humorless laugh. "I am more inclined to trust the ravens we just saw than I am to trust anything coming out of that red reptile's lips."

Cheyanne nodded. She hesitated a moment, then asked, "Can you still hear her? In the silver?"

Lisbet considered it. "Not like before," she said, finally. "Not the horrific screaming. Now it is more... a steadying presence, almost a resolve. Somehow she senses we are coming. She is waiting for us." Suddenly she looked up at Cheyanne. "I truly wish you had not come. You must see now that this... whatever it is... it cannot have anything to do with your own heritage."

"I don't see that at all," Cheyanne said, stung. "And I thought you liked having me here. You said—"

"I'm saying *now* that we are all in danger," Lisbet cut in. "I'm saying we might die. Do you understand that?"

Cheyanne was still hurt, but the fear and sadness in Doctor Lisbet's words curbed her impulse to argue. Instead, she said in a small voice, "I just want to help."

Lisbet's eyes slitted. "I know," she said, finally. "But we may have reached a point where your presence will be a liability. We cannot give hostages to... To whatever the power is that holds Anne-Marie in its grip. I fear for your own soul as well as hers. Do you understand?"

"Yes." Cheyanne said. "I won't get in the way. If we get to a place where you tell me I can't go further I will obey you, I promise." She stuck her chin out. "But we aren't there yet."

"Hell, Lisbet, if she ain't yourn she might as well be." Fallon's chuckle came from behind them. "Look at that chin out, same as you do when your dander's up."

It surprised both Lisbet and Cheyanne into laughter. "Damn you, Jonas," Lisbet said, smiling. "Must you always be joking? I was trying to have a serious talk with her."

"Serious talking. I see." Fallon grinned. "Well, then, seriously, Lisbet, the kid's been a help several times. She's bringing fresh eyes to all our old miseries from the abbey and it's been good for us. She's old enough to make her own decision and you raised her right. So's you should relax." He raised an eyebrow at Cheyanne. "And you, youngster, you listen to Lisbet. She ain't wrong about what we might be riding into."

"Well, what *are* we riding into?" This was Brainerd. He glared at them, then turned to include Aaron in the glare as well.

"Trouble." Fallon grunted. "Apart from that you know as much as any of us do, Nels. So we might as well eat something and rest up so's we're ready for it."

• • •

Dinner was a simple matter of dried meat and fruit from the supplies Coretta had packed for them. There was no wood to make a fire, so they spread out the bedrolls in a line huddled together at the base of the cliff, opposite the pool. Cheyanne and Brainerd tied the horses and mules to a jagged bit of boulder a little way further on, making sure the animals had enough slack to move around a little. She said to him, "When were you in Hyacinth, anyway?"

"Long time ago. Before Stonegarden. Just passing through, really. I was... traveling." He shrugged. "Thought I might stop there for awhile, actually, it wasn't a bad little place. But there was some troubles."

"A woman?"

"Now you sound just like Lisbet." The blond man snorted. "I ain't always thinking about going after some woman, you know. Else I wouldn't be on this fool's crusade." He raised an eyebrow. "What's it to you?"

"It's one of the few places I remember my mother talking about," Cheyanne said. "I think she might have been from that part of the country."

"You ain't Lisbet's?" Brainerd was surprised. "I figured... well, actually,

I never gave it much thought but now you mention it I can't see any man taming Lisbet enough to… well, never mind." He flashed a sheepish grin that Cheyanne couldn't help smiling at in return. "How the hell you end up with her then?"

"My mama died on her operating table. Doctor Lisbet took me in after."

"Course she did. Lost causes n' fool crusades. She collects em like treasures. Shoulda known." Brainerd hawked and spat. "No daddy anywhere to be found, I'm guessing."

"Doctor Lisbet says it's better not to depend on a man. That it's a trap for womenfolk."

"Course she does. I daresay if your daddy showed up Lisbet would give him such a spitting-mad talking to it'd flay the hide off him." Brainerd snorted at the thought. "I imagine she'll have you trained up to be the same kind of scary bitch she is, soon enough. Assuming we live though what's coming." He let out a small bark of laughter. "Don't mind me, kid. We're all just the devil's fools, now. You and me and Lisbet and all of us. Nothing to do but play out the string."

● ● ●

Cheyanne awoke with a start.

There was no light in the hollow between the cliffs where they had camped, and she could not see the danger that was upon them. But she knew it was there—rather, her body did, tense and shuddering with the reflexes of flight. She heard the rustle of movement from the others, and down the canyon was the noise of an animal snarling…no, more than one. Many. Getting closer.

Doctor Lisbet's hand clamped on her arm. She whispered, "Steady, little one. You must be still."

"What is it?" Cheyanne's whisper was quavering.

"Coyotes. Or wolves. A pack of them. Hunting. They must smell us." Lisbet released Cheyanne's arm and she could feel the doctor fumbling in the saddlebags they were using as an improvised pillow. "We shall have to shoot one or two of them, frighten the others off."

"Way ahead of you, doc." This was Brainerd. They could barely see him in the shadows under the cliff, until suddenly the muzzle flash from his pistol lit his face in sharp relief as he fired. And fired again. And again, and again. Then from the other side Lisbet's .32 fired as well.

The snarls from the shadows deepened in intensity and Cheyanne thought she saw a golden glow coming from further down the path. The air around them seemed to thicken somehow, and she realized that Fallon and Doctor Lisbet were using the Language.

"It's no good, gorgeous." Fallon's voice. "Glamour's not taking. Guns won't stop 'em either. Somebody messed with them animals. See the gold on them? Aura? They been juiced up somehow. Someone using the Language out here besides us."

"Someone sent them, then? For us?" Aaron's voice.

"Must have." Fallon's voice was hard and clipped. "Later for the whys, now's not the time. Nels, Lisbet, you keep firing down there whilst me and Aaron get Larry and Miss Cheyanne mounted up. We can't lose the horses. Come on now, move!"

There was no argument, not even from Brainerd. Cheyanne could see the yellow light coming towards them from the other end of the cleft, where it had first opened out into the gorge, and silhouetted in front of it, Brainerd and Doctor Lisbet standing ready, guns out. She hastily gathered up the bedrolls, thanking God that none of them had bothered with undressing. She had Sultan and Isobel saddled in moments as Fallon and Aaron struggled to muscle the semi-conscious form of Lawrence's body on to Fallon's Girl. "I'll take him, Aaron," she heard Fallon saying. "We ain't got time to rig the mules. Mine'll take double. You fetch Nels and Lisbet now. Cheyanne! Get Sultan over here. Come on girl, we gotta move." She wasn't sure whether Fallon meant her or the horse but it didn't matter.

There was more shooting. Then hoofbeats and somehow, in the velvet darkness, they were moving. Isobel was badly spooked now from the growls and gunshots and it was all Cheyanne could do to keep from falling off. She would just have to trust that the pony would know where it was going.

They emerged from the cleft out on to relatively open country. The light was better out here, the moon was still up, and her eyes were adjusting. She saw Lisbet and Sultan galloping out behind her, and Brainerd bringing up the rear, twisted into an impossible posture in the saddle as he managed to guide his rawboned Palouse with reins clutched in one fist while facing rearward, still firing at the wolf pack chasing them. "Gunshots ain't doing shit," he bellowed. "Not even slowing them down."

"Enhanced, then," Lisbet huffed, still somewhat out of breath. "Jonas! Can we—"

"Already doing it, Lisbet." Fallon was not shouting but his voice carried to all of them nevertheless. "With me, now, all of you. Close in. Not sure how far I can prop us up. Lisbet, Aaron, help me out here."

Cheyanne had no idea what he meant but she could again feel the charge of the Language building around them. The air shimmered. Isobel whinnied in fear and shied, but her hooves met nothing but air. Yet somehow they were still moving, forward, towards the distant hills.

"Lisbet, Aaron, Nels, help me dammit, I can't carry us all." This was in the eerie layered tones Cheyanne had heard from Lisbet before, only this time it was Fallon's voice. The air felt thicker around them, almost gelatinous. Below, she could see the sand and scrub speeding beneath them in a blur, as though they were on a railroad train, yet Isobel's hooves hardly moved.

"I am trying, Jonas. But the wolves are still with us. There, and there." Lisbet's voice was echoing and strange. But even so, Cheyanne heard the fear in it. *"Try to find a place of concealment—perhaps a glamour will shield us this time."*

"They're herding us, damn it. Toward the ridge." Brainerd's voice was layered as well, but somehow more brittle than the others. *"Like—*oh hell, look out, they're…!" His voice lost its Hermetic echo and suddenly the air cleared around them and they were surrounded by growling, snapping wolves, their eyes glowing an ugly yellow with unnatural light. The horses' gliding movement stopped so abruptly that Cheyanne was almost thrown. The others reined up and stared at the wolf pack surrounding them.

"What the hell?" Fallon pulled up on the big bay and wheeled to face them, Lawrence's unconscious form draped over his lap. "Everyone all right? Aaron, you still with us?"

"Ayuh." Aaron's voice was panting with exertion. "Why ain't they attacking?"

"Wondering that m'self," Fallon said. "They woke us up and chased us out here and for what? Just to sit?"

"How far we get, anyhow?" Brainerd wanted to know. "Way you all was carrying us we musta made at least five, ten miles just running blind. Seems like we just got more lost. I got no damn idea where we—"

Doctor Lisbet pointed. "There, gentlemen. At the foot of the ridge, ahead of us. I think we have arrived."

The others all turned to see a cavern opening in the cliff ahead, maybe thirty yards beyond where the wolves held them. An eerie yellow light pulsed from deep within.

"Fine." Brainerd's face twisted into an angry scowl. He slid off his Palouse and checked the loads in his pistol. "Let's start the ball."

The others dismounted as well. Fallon looked at Brainerd and snorted.

"Holster that iron, you idjit. Guns ain't going to do us any good here, that's obvious."

Lisbet looked back at the wolves, then towards the glow from the cave ahead. She sighed. "This would be where I would tell you to wait, little one," she said to Cheyanne. "But not with these animals out here. Just... stay close to me."

Cheyanne nodded. They walked slowly toward the cave.

A silhouette fell over the golden light coming from the opening. "You're here. At last." A cackling, brittle laugh.

They halted, waiting. A figure floated out of the cave toward them.

It was a woman, her face ravaged with sores and lesions. Her eyes glowed a spectral green. Her clothing was torn and stained with clay. Cheyanne became aware of a hideous smell, something like sulfur and damp earth and rotted meat, but none of those were exactly right. It made her feel nauseous and it was hard to look at the ruined face grinning at them out of the yellow light. She could feel Lisbet's hand clamp on to her shoulder, pulling her back.

"No, no, Lisbet, let her loose. Your little Kuyagah girl's the guest of honor tonight. When the ravens told me you planned to leave her behind I had to send the wolves for you." The floating woman laughed again. "My, but that was a ride, wasn't it?"

Abruptly Brainerd stepped forward and fired his pistol point-blank at the woman. Twice, three times, again and again until he had fired the gun empty.

Nothing happened. The floating woman scowled at him. "Not nice," she said. Suddenly Brainerd was doubled over, screaming. He collapsed on to the sand.

Cheyanne ran to him. He was still breathing and she thought she could hear him mutter the word *bitch*. She stood and faced the floating figure and snapped, "All right! We're here! You don't have to hurt anyone! What do you want? Who *are* you?"

"Who d'you think?" Brainerd gasped, trying to sit up. "It's her. Anne-Marie. She done played us again."

• • •

Ten

Mistress of the Obsidian (Anne-Marie's Story)

Anne-Marie had come to the desert because it was her destiny.

At least, that was what Ezekiel had always said and she believed him. "One day you will be called upon to be the savior of mankind," he assured her. "You must remain pure of body and of purpose. We have great work ahead of us."

When the old man had first come to the California mining camp in his black wagon, she had been a little afraid of him. She had been only a girl of nine, then, but she had already learned how to manipulate and divert her father from taking out his misery on her. Her mother had died of complications following Anne-Marie's birth and she knew that her father blamed her for it somehow. He never said so—well, except when he was drunk—but as the years passed and the mine started to play out and life became continually harder, she could feel her father's hatred more and more. She dreamed of someone who would come and take her away to a better life, a life where she could be loved and safe and happy. She never dreamed that it would be the man with the white beard and the pale blue eyes, pulling up in his black wagon.

"My daddy's not home yet," she said. "He had to go to the diggings."

He had looked at her very hard for a long time. "Not many left here."

"Daddy says there's another vein of pure going to open up soon and all he has to do is find it. Then we'll be living better." She said it like a catechism, the way her daddy always said it.

"Do you believe that?"

Anne-Marie nodded, but there was doubt in her eyes.

The old man looked at her for another long moment, then something in his face changed. He had made up his mind. He climbed down from the wagon and smiled, and suddenly she wasn't afraid of him at all. "Tell me about your dreams, child."

Anne-Marie hesitated. "Daddy doesn't like it," she said at last.

"Your daddy doesn't understand them, but I bet I will. You dream of

"My daddy's not home yet."

black birds, don't you? And a ring of stones in the desert. A place of great power. Yes?"

Her eyes grew wide. "That's exactly it! And a pool made out of—it's not water—it's like a rock, it's made out of dark glass! But you can still go inside it—"

"Yes. That is the obsidian, my dear." The old man's eyes glittered with triumph. "You are the girl I have been looking for. You are chosen." He paused. "Your mama… she was not a white woman."

"I never knew her. Daddy said she was from over the mountains. The high desert."

"Yes." The old man nodded. "That is where I am going, child, the home of your mother's people. I think you can help me find it."

"How?"

"With your dreams." The old man knelt before her so they were eye to eye. "You are very special, and … you must understand this. Dreams sent me to you. As you dreamed of the birds and the glass pool, so I have dreamed of the girl that is to be the obsidian's princess. That's you, little lady, and I have been looking for you for ever so long. Come with me. You know your daddy doesn't want you. Leave him to his anger and his drinking. Come with me and be a princess." He held out his arms to her.

Anne-Marie didn't even have to think it over. "Oh, yes!" she breathed, and as he gathered her to him and lifted her to the wagon she thought she might burst from sheer happiness.

He climbed up beside her and twitched the reins, and they started back down the mountain.

Anne-Marie beamed up at the old man. "What's your name, mister?"

"I am Ezekiel." He grinned. "Same as the prophet. And I see a magical future for you, my dear."

She nodded, hardly daring to believe it could be so, but still wanting to, so much. "Honest injun?" she whispered.

"Ha!" This made Ezekiel laugh and laugh. At first she thought he was laughing at her, but he put his hand on her head and affectionately tousled her hair. "Yes, indeed, my dear. *Honest injun,*" and then he chuckled again and put his arm around her.

● ● ●

That was how it began. Ezekiel taught her a great deal—reading and writing and history and mathematics, to start, and by her twelfth year he had also given her the rudiments of the Language. "What I have is fragmentary," he admitted. "Until we find the obsidian temple itself, we must blunder along as best we can."

Anne-Marie didn't mind. She was happy just to be with him, to be loved and to belong to someone.

As she grew into young womanhood, though, she began to look at Ezekiel with different eyes and speculate about their future. Traveling all over the eastern Oregon territory and even sometimes Idaho, casting around in the high desert country for the rocks they both saw in dreams now... it began to feel futile and empty to Anne-Marie. She had long ago abandoned her childish fantasy about becoming an Indian princess, and she knew that her mother's tribe was largely extinct. But that was all right.

What gnawed at her was how Ezekiel always kept his distance. He was affectionate, certainly, but there was always a wall between them and it frustrated her terribly. She loved him and he loved her and that should mean that they should be married, shouldn't it? But when she brought up the subject—strictly as an abstract, wondering what it would be like to have a husband, Ezekiel snorted and said there were far better things in store for her.

One night, shortly after her sixteenth birthday, as they sat around their campfire, she made him laugh with her exaggerated growling imitation of the man who ran the general store in Grants Pass. He hugged her and before he could pull away, she leaned in and kissed him, hard.

For a moment—a half-second, no more—she felt him respond, then he thrust her away from him and stood, panting. "What are you doing?"

"What do you think?" She smiled, teasing, trying to recapture the good humor of a minute ago. "You're a learned man, you should know what it means when a girl kisses a fella like that."

For the first time she could remember, Ezekiel looked genuinely angry. "You must never, ever do that. Ever. You have a destiny."

"What? To be a princess? Be serious, Zeke. Look at this." She waved a hand at the wagon and the campfire. "Princess of what? We haven't found your temple and we probably never will. So what? We're happy, aren't we? Why can't we settle for that? Live and be happy? Why are we still looking? The dreams don't tell us anything we don't know. Desert country. We've been all over the deserts everywhere we can find, and a bunch of forests too. What's the—"

As she spoke, his expression had darkened with anger, and suddenly golden light erupted from Ezekiel's hands. Her words stopped and she could not get her breath. She struggled to speak, to form the Language that would free her but she was choking, he was *killing* her.

Abruptly the glow faded and she collapsed to the ground. She looked up at him, her eyes filling with tears. "What is *wrong* with what—"

"I looked for you for eleven years! All over this world—here, Europe, even China!" The old man's voice was grating with suppressed rage. "You are the one! The gateway can only be opened by one who is pure, who can be the bride that will carry the seed! You are chosen for far better things than—"

"But I love *you!*" She was crying openly now. "Why is that so wrong? You love me too, don't you?"

This stopped him. For a moment Ezekiel's face twisted with a bitter awareness, then he smiled ruefully. "Of course I do. But we cannot... we are so close now, my dear. I know we are. The visions—they begin to come in daylight now, we can see the auras of living things and the lines of energy in the earth. These will guide us. We are... we must be true to our purpose. We are the last hope. If the obsidian is to be awakened and your— our—destiny fulfilled, we must not give in to our weaknesses. We *must* not." He paused. "Swear to me. And I will swear to you."

Anne-Marie nodded, not trusting herself to speak without weeping. She had planned this night, this moment, for weeks now, and it was a disaster. Not only did he not want her, but he acted like she had betrayed him. Now he would not trust her again ever, unless she took this oath. For reasons she still did not understand.

But it was important to him and she loved him, in spite of everything. So she nodded and said softly, "I swear."

Ezekiel nodded. "Good. And I swear to you. We shall not speak of this again."

Anne-Marie nodded.

But she thought of it, many times. Of how wonderful it had been for that brief moment, when he had given in to his feelings and kissed her back. Some day... some day she would have that again with a man. That was the real oath she swore that night.

Two days later, Aaron joined them.

● ● ●

Ten days after that, they found the obsidian.

Ezekiel was almost giddy. "After all these long years," he breathed. His smile was wider than Anne-Marie had ever seen it. "To look upon it… now, truly, we shall make a new beginning. This will become a garden."

Aaron was unable to look at the pool of glass shards for long, even obscured by the circle of runestones around it. Instead, he stood with his back to it and surveyed the canyon below and the bleak cliffs of chalk and granite above. "Garden of rocks, maybe. Ain't even soil here. Just sand."

"A garden of stones, then!" Anne-Marie's cheer felt forced to her, and the remark held a sly dig at Ezekiel's unreasoning joy, but neither Ezekiel or Aaron seemed to notice.

Aaron snorted. "Can't eat rocks. Guess I better see what I can rustle up for us for dinner, if this is where we're stoppin'." He paused. "We aren't bedding down right next to… whatever that is." He waved a vague hand at the runestone circle. "Are we?"

Ezekiel abruptly noticed him. "It is unsettling for you. It makes you ill to look upon. Of course. You don't have the Language." He considered it, then pointed. "We can move the wagon down that way a little, and picket the horses there. Eventually we shall have to build a façade of some kind."

"We'll need help for that." Aaron looked relieved at discussing practical matters. "Supplies too. Tools. Nails and wood."

"Canyon City is not far. A few days' ride. As for help… others will come." Ezekiel looked serenely at him, then back at the obsidian.

Aaron waited. When no further words came, he shrugged, winked at Anne-Marie, then shouldered Ezekiel's long rifle and trudged down the path the way they came. "Dinner first. I'll get the wagon in a bit."

As he disappeared down the trail, Anne-Marie looked at Ezekiel. "It hurts him to be here. We need to give him the Language too."

"Child!" The shock served to divert Ezekiel's attention from the runestones. "You cannot be serious. His race—his people are not genetically capable. Even among whites there are only a few for whom—"

"The only race with a genetic advantage for the Language is Kuyagah," she snapped back, stung. "You said so yourself."

"I had not thought it necessary to point out that lesser races would be exempt." Ezekiel sniffed, then smiled. "Your compassion does you credit. But you must never forget the larger duty we must fulfill. You have a destiny."

It was then that Ezekiel lost her, though neither one of them fully realized it.

• • •

In the coming weeks, others did indeed join them. First Fallon, then Larry and Theo. Philip came later, after almost a year. By then they had completed the façade surrounding the stones, three cabins, and a stable for the horses. One night Anne-Marie dubbed their little conclave of wooden buildings "Stonegarden Abbey" as a joke, but it stuck. Even Ezekiel began to refer to the place that way.

Anne-Marie by this time could read auras as easily as a normal person can see hair color. She realized that hers must be as obvious and it chilled her to think that Ezekiel might see her thoughts reflected in it. She began to use the Language as a cloak, learning how to use Hermetics to shape her own somatic responses, subtly changing the rest of her physical self as well as her brain.

The result was a sort of enhancement of her health and reflexes that felt like a constant low thrumming of power throughout her body. But more importantly, the golden glow that this brought upon her obscured her aura from the others and especially from Ezekiel. He must never know that she had used the ravens to summon these specific members of their company, sending her winged servants to scout the surrounding country. She had sought out, not so much like-minded companions with a potential aptitude with the Language as Ezekiel had wished her to do, but instead— though she hardly dared admit it to herself—people with qualities that could help should it ever come to a showdown with Ezekiel. Fallon was an experienced scout and rider and he had been a soldier. Larry and Theo were very good at ferreting out personal information and reading people. Lisbet was a healer. And Philip... Philip was because she was lonely.

Anne-Marie still loved Ezekiel, and she knew that he loved her in his way. But she also knew that he was not truly capable of love, not the kind she craved. They were all gaining powers and abilities beyond normal humans, but Ezekiel was leaving humanity itself behind him. His quest was somehow to merge with the obsidian, to open a gateway to the dimension described on the runestones. As such he considered love a weakness, another symptom of human frailty.

She knew now that she would never have him, and she was forming a bond with Aaron that was almost more profound than the one she shared with Ezekiel. But of course Ezekiel was blind to Aaron most of the time. He never noticed the cook's extraordinary intelligence, his intuitive grasp of the personalities and the dynamic of the group, and he was the only one whom Anne-Marie felt she could truly confide in. But she could not *be* with Aaron, not in the way she longed for. Not without giving up everything else.

Philip was her first try at threading the needle, at finding a man that Ezekiel would approve of, and thus she could have it all. As the weeks passed she began to think it an acceptable compromise, though she did not feel the closeness with him that came so naturally with Aaron.

Then, suddenly, it was over. One morning Ezekiel took her aside and said, "This thing with Philip. End it."

She protested, "What thing—there is no thing!" But she knew what he meant. Philip was in love with her. He was not hiding it. She did not love him in return, but she did like him, and she had thought that, perhaps, in time...

However, Ezekiel clearly was not going to give her the time. "You know what I am talking about. He is obsessed with you. He hoped you would come to him of your own will but you have been toying with him, leading him—"

"I like him! He is good company, he has been a perfect gentleman, brilliant, chivalrous... how can you object to such a man?" She did not add, *It could have been you but you scorned me... what did you expect?*

The jealousy she hoped was behind his words did not show in Ezekiel's face. He just said, "You have a *destiny*."

Her heart sank. "That is your answer to everything!" *Of course he's not jealous. He can only see his dreams.*

"It is the *reason* for everything." Ezekiel was unmoved by her anger. But then his voice softened a little. "I know it is hard for you sometimes. But you must... you must be patient. You must be pure."

She could only stare at him, her anger and humiliation fighting with her love for Ezekiel and, yes, for Philip a little. It swirled in a whirlpool of emotion inside her, choking off her words. She could feel tears welling.

Ezekiel took her silence for assent and nodded. "He'll be gone by afternoon. It's done." He abruptly turned on his heel and left her standing in the clearing between the cabins, headed back to the abbey façade and the obsidian. That damned obsidian.

Her first thought was to seek out Philip and warn him, apologize, help him to flee... from what? She wasn't sure, but there was something in the resolve Ezekiel showed on his face... Philip was in danger now. She knew it.

She turned and saw her ravens there; they had sensed her inner turmoil and sought to serve her. Seven of them had lighted on the crude shingles of the roof of the cabin behind her... the one where Lisbet slept. Without thinking, her hands shaped the energies in the air and her lips formed words in the ancient tongue. *Find a warrior, a man well-schooled in the arts of death. He must love and obey me without question. Find him now.*

The birds took to the air. Anne-Marie still had no plan, not really—just the need to find Philip and warn him somehow. She reached out now, not with her physical senses but her ethereal ones, seeking Philip's aura.

The knowledge came back almost at once... he was close, very close. Good God, he was in the abbey building! With Ezekiel!

She whirled and ran up the gravel path to the wooden building that housed the runestone circle. As she reached for the door there was a sudden wave of pressure and pain that almost caused her to cry out. Not physical pain, exactly, though she did feel a physical reaction. It felt like something... cruel. Conscious and malevolent. The sheer force of it doubled her over and she almost vomited. She stood, panting, until the dizziness passed.

She quailed for a moment and almost ran back the way she came. Then she remembered Philip. She couldn't just leave him, though she wanted nothing more than to curl up into a ball and whimper. Nevertheless, shaking and nauseated, she moved forward to the abbey facade. Slowly.

Still woozy, she opted for caution. Instead of bursting in and confronting Ezekiel as she had originally planned to, she just opened the door a crack, enough for a peek.

Ezekiel stood inside the runestone circle, almost at the edge of the pool of obsidian chips. He was smiling with beatitude at Philip, who was standing waist-deep in the pool.

But he was not Philip, not any longer. His eyes were empty, and his skin... as she watched, it rippled and changed, becoming scarlet and scaly. His mouth opened and though his face remained empty of expression, his voice was tinged with hoarse panic. "Wait...please. I'm... narrrrrgh—" It stopped being words and degenerated into a low, throaty moan. Then silence.

"Better now?" Ezekiel was still smiling. "Then you understand at last. You have served, you see. Azathoth must feed, and Shabbat-Ka. Soon will come the time when all will be restored. But in the meantime, go now and sleep until I call you again. Your sacrifice is great and it is appreciated. Know that you have given them the first of many."

Philip, or the red empty form that had replaced him, nodded. Slowly he sank into the pool of black glass chips until nothing was visible.

Anne-Marie slowly closed the door to the abbey and stood for a moment, shaking.

At first she could only think of flight. She ran to the stable and saddled Sultan, muttering a few words of the Language to ensure his footing along the cliffs. In no time at all they were galloping toward the canyon path that led away from Stonegarden, Sultan fairly flying along the road with his Hermetic enhancement.

A few minutes later she saw the ravens returning. *They had found a warrior, he was coming up the path.* Then she saw Jonas and Lisbet, out for their walk. She pivoted and rode for them, anxious to tell them…

…tell them what? What had she seen? She knew that they were dealing with powerful and unknown forces. And what had Ezekiel said? Certainly, it was not a threat; he had been pleased with Philip, if anything. Was Philip perhaps… had he *volunteered* for… that? Could she be wrong? About everything? Was Ezekiel's anger directed not at her but at the possibility that she could have ruined whatever he had planned for Philip?

How could she doubt the man who had given her so much?

All this skittered though her mind in barely a second, just as she and Sultan came galloping up past where Jonas and Lisbet stood talking. It was then that she saw the other man and her heart leapt with hope. The ravens told her this was who she sought… Nels, his name was.

So this was her warrior. Her handsome shootist. Well, the ravens had brought him and now he was hers, might as well make the best of it. What happened with Philip…it would be best just to let that lie. See what Ezekiel said when they returned.

She might have been wrong. She *must* be wrong. Ezekiel could not have forced Philip to sacrifice himself to…to whatever it was in the pool.

Because then… the things he had said… that might mean he planned to sacrifice them all.

● ● ●

With Philip gone and Nels settling in, life at Stonegarden soon returned to its regular routine of studies in the morning and campfire merriment at night, and in the following weeks Anne-Marie persuaded herself that she was worrying over nothing. Ezekiel seemed to be his usual self and none of the others were behaving in any way other than expected. It was easy to imagine that she must have somehow got it wrong about what she had seen with Ezekiel and Philip and the obsidian.

This inner compromise was aided by the Hermetic power that pulsed through her nearly all the time now. It gave her confidence and a feeling of well-being that sometimes bordered on giddiness. She had begun as an act of camouflage, to hide her aura, but she found that channeling Hermetic energy was pleasurable for its own sake. Her communication and control over the ravens and other beasts was becoming as easy as speaking in plain English, and though no one noticed, her feet rarely even touched the ground any more. Rather, Anne-Marie glided everywhere now, floating a quarter-inch to a half-inch in the air, riding the golden energy the way a twig rides the rapids in a river. She knew that her companions were beginning to wonder about her.

All but Nels, of course. He was too devoted. Though she knew it was in some sense artificial, created by her own Hermetic command, still it was a comfort to her. They would ride out together in the afternoons and sit and look over the canyon below them, often with her nestled comfortably in his brawny arms. Sometimes he would kiss her and she would let him, but when he reached for her, she gently slid away. Her control over him was such that he never protested.

Until the last time, when he merely shook his head and reached again, pulling her to him, crushing her. She squeaked in protest and then his lips were on hers again and she was *struggling*, he was *forcing* her…

…but she did not need the Language now, really, or even the gestures. She was saturated with the golden power and when she thought **STOP**, he froze.

Indeed, he was so unmoving that it was difficult for her to slide out of the hug he held her in, but she did not dare remove the geas she had laid on him until she was free. So she squirmed and huffed until, finally, she emerged disheveled and sweaty from under his arms. She pulled the shoulder of her blouse back into place and looked at his motionless form for a moment, his unshaven face with the mouth twisted with desire, contrasting with the empty eyes as the geas held him. If Nels was not truly her creature, if his will was reasserting itself… could she trust him? Could she trust anyone?

Suddenly her old fears all came crashing back on her. What she had seen with Ezekiel, and Philip. And now Nels was becoming a different sort of threat.

Should she flee? The power was within her, her entire being suffused with the golden glow; she did not need the obsidian or even the Language any more. But would the others… what if their loyalty to Ezekiel was such… she would have to find out. A truth spell. At the evening gathering, that would be best. If any of the others were allied with Ezekiel in his plans, she would know.

She mounted Sultan and started back to the compound, thoughtful. As she rode, she wondered what it would be like to leave, to be alone for the first time in her life, and shuddered. Even with the power, the thought frightened her. She thought of Aaron. Maybe the two of them could... but no. The world would not permit it.

She glanced over her shoulder, decided she was safely away, and fluttered a hand, releasing Brainerd from his trance. She was weeping as she and Sultan reached the top of the ridge.

• • •

The evening did not go well. Certainly, it did not go as she planned.

Theo's homemade wine had changed easily, with a pass of her hands. But the truths that came out afterward, even though clearly many of the company were as nervous about Ezekiel as she was herself... nevertheless those revelations were not at all reassuring. Worst of all was when Lawrence suddenly turned on her in frustrated rage. Because he could not lie, the harsh words he spat at her were all the more embarrassing and hateful. So she fled in tears.

She loved them all but she dared trust none of them. The entire group was fragile, cracking at the edges. They might even blame her. After all, she had brought each of them here with her ravens, hadn't she? Perhaps the friendship she felt for them and they for her... maybe it was all just Hermetic artifact, a false consequence of the golden power humming within her. The only one she was sure of any more was Aaron.

Very well, then, she would go to Aaron. It was all ending anyway, she could feel it. Why not? She loved him—the wine had worked on her as well, and there was no denying her deep feeling for the gentle camp cook rising uppermost in her consciousness. That was how the spell was constructed, to bring the hidden truths of the self to the surface.

"I do love him," she whispered. "Noth—" she stopped and choked.

She had started to assure herself, *Nothing else matters*. But she couldn't say it. It was a lie. The wine would not permit her to utter the words.

"I don't care," she said. "I'm going anyway."

She could say that, so she knew it was true. Reassured, she knocked on Aaron's cabin door, and when he opened it, she fell into his arms.

• • •

The next day, the joy in her heart at finding Aaron loved her in return,along with the Hermetic power she bathed in all the time now, combined to create a sort of euphoria that made her fears seem like the sheerest foolishness. It was all going to be fine. She floated through the day feeling invulnerable in her newfound love, not daring to be alone with Aaron for a second because she knew she would cover him with kisses, and even in her bubbly happiness she knew that it was not yet something to share with the others. It seemed an eternity until the sun went down and she could go to him again. For a moment she even considered speeding time to make the night come faster, but she restrained herself.

Inside the golden thrum of Hermetic energy where she floated almost constantly, her vision had altered over the last few weeks to where she saw the temporal and biological energies surrounding everything the way a normal human saw a waterfall. She was certain that she could shape time now in the same way she shaped the energy of the physical world, but that was far too much power to unleash; the manipulation of time was something even she had not yet dared to experiment with, though she thought Ezekiel might have. In a distant, academic way, she thought she might not even be truly human any longer, but something different, something *better*. She would teach this to Aaron and then the others and they would all live happily here in Stonegarden forever. Surely this must have been what Ezekiel and Philip had been seeking in the obsidian. She was a fool to have ever doubted. Then her thoughts returned to Aaron and what they had shared, and a shudder of ecstasy went through her. She would tell all this to him tonight... but after. Loving him would be first. There would be time enough later for the rest.

Night finally came. She fairly flew to Aaron's cabin and into his arms, and it was the same glorious thing again. But afterward...when she was about to confide her hopes to him... just like the wine, it all went wrong.

First Nels burst in on them with murder in his eyes. Terrified he was going to kill them both, Anne-Marie had lashed out and wiped his memories, adding a command for him to leave Stonegarden.

But then Aaron shocked her by saying he wanted to leave, as well. He told her he had heard Jonas and Lisbet talking about something Ezekiel had hidden from them. About the true purpose of the obsidian. It was some sort of blockade or prison for otherworldly beings... "emissaries," Lisbet had said. And Ezekiel was going to free these things by sacrificing them all.

She didn't want to believe it, but even inside her happiness she knew it was true. He asked her to run, said the others were leaving as well.

It would not be enough. Running by itself would not insure their safety. And none of the others had the capability to stop her mentor. None of the others could see what she could. She looked at Aaron and in that moment, she knew what she had to do.

She told him to wait while she went for the horses, making some excuse about Sultan. It was flimsy and absurd, especially considering she had almost total control over the local wildlife at this point, but Aaron did not argue. She dressed quickly and, with a final kiss, told Aaron she would be back soon and went out into the night.

Anne-Marie could see the air rippling around the buildings as she emerged into the moonlight, and then as her eyes adjusted she saw Larry kneeling on the path over what looked like a red bag of clothing. Then Larry abruptly stood and ran into the abbey. As she got closer to the form on the path she could see that it was Theo, or what was left of him.

He was dead. The surrounding sand was sticky with congealed blood, shining burgundy under the pale moonlight. His body had been flayed and torn as though a hundred whips had been at him at once. But she knew it had not been whips, or even the claws of an animal. It had been the obsidian. She whirled and ran up the path to the wooden façade of the abbey.

As she burst in she could see Ezekiel himself, stripped to the waist and standing knee-deep in the pool of broken black glass. He held Lawrence floating helpless in a golden halo before him, oblivious to Anne-Marie's entrance and her horrified expression.

"You murdered him. We trusted you… I loved you. Theo knew it and he knew… it was destroying us… and you murdered him." Lawrence's voice was strangled, a drowning man's plea. "Why? He only wanted you to let us leave. He was trying… trying to save me. Save us. From you. You are a murderer."

"I killed no one!" Ezekiel was screaming. "He did it to himself! Theo defied the very source of our power! You dare to speak of destruction! He came here and sought to destroy Azathoth! To defile everything we have worked for these last two years! Of course the obsidian destroyed him!"

"What are you doing? Stop it! *Stop it right now!*" Anne-Marie's words came out in a shriek layered with Hermetic power.

It staggered Ezekiel. The glow around Lawrence faded and his body fell to the sand, just short of the pool of black glass. She saw that the pool was no longer made of chips and shards of the black mineral but had morphed into a black liquid veined with gold. It rippled like a living thing, tendrils made of glittering black and gold rising and then subsuming back into the larger pool. Anne-Marie could feel a sense of dull hunger flowing from it—no, from behind it, like something pushing to get through. It reached out a questing pod for Lawrence and as it touched him she saw something shimmer around him, his life was being pulled from him, leaving a scaly red husk of a body behind.

In her horror at this sight she had forgotten Ezekiel. And she had forgotten to mask her aura. Suddenly she heard him scream. "You little whore! You were to give yourself to Azathoth—you were to be the one to carry his seed—and instead you gave yourself to that son of mud? You debased yourself with—"

"I gave myself to you! I gave you my life and I wanted to give you my love! You refused it! You betrayed us all!" Her anger merged with the golden power. It gave her strength and amplified her emotion into a physical thing. She floated a foot or so above the ground, again bathed in light. Without even thinking about it she directed it at Ezekiel in a searing bolt that lifted him clear out of the black pool and flung him against the circle of runestones, shattering them.

But the bearded man was merely startled. He too now glowed with a halo of otherworldly energy. "You foolish child. I am immortal now. I will begin again. It might take another century but I will bring forth the old ones. I have been given their wisdom now; I know exactly what is needed. There are other girls. I know now that it must be Kuyagah." He struggled awkwardly to his feet and smiled. "And you—"

Anne-Marie was suddenly aware of a dark presence *inside* her, the questing black tendrils of the obsidian reaching for her on the ethereal plane as well as the physical. And she could feel Ezekiel there as well. *Inside her mind.*

She screamed in sheer animal terror. With the Hermetic power that flowed through her she reached for the essence of the cliffside itself, wrenching at it in an effort to bring it all down on Ezekiel and the thing in the pool, squelch it, push it away, bury it forever. The ground shuddered and split and she could feel fire boiling up from the bowels of the earth. *Yes. Fire. Fire will kill anything.* She could feel all the cabins around them bursting into flames. *No, here,* she thought. She pulled at it and aimed it at Ezekiel and suddenly they were in an inferno. As fire swirled around the golden sphere of power around them, Anne-Marie could see his skin blacken and crisp. She felt a brief moment of triumph. But then he was no

"You little whore!"

longer in his dying body, he was fully inside her mind…

She had only one option left. She stopped time for the two of them and there was a silent scream of fury from Ezekiel. He was slowed, almost paralyzed, but even inside the frozen moment he was still grasping for her, trying to crush her essence with his own. *He's killing me! Stop him, stop him before…* She screamed, not with her voice but with her very essence, reaching out to the rest of the group, her true family, the people she had called to her and then come to love. She felt Lisbet out on the canyon ridge astride Sultan; Fallon struggling to reach the abbey as the air and earth itself rippled insanely around him; Aaron standing by the stables, helpless and grieving; even Nels out on the trail halfway to Canyon City and poor inert Larry lying red and empty on the sand. *Save me. Save me. I can't fight him.*

Before her, the charred form of her mentor was still trying to move. Ezekiel's lips cracked and split as they pulled away from his teeth in a silent snarl.

Still not dead then… Anne-Marie flung her essence outward in one last panicked effort with everything she had and there was a bright flash of silver as the earth split beneath them. They fell and kept falling; her, Ezekiel, the roiling cluster of obsidian, all of it under an avalanche of granite and sand and everything that made up the cliffs they were on, a sinkhole that went down and down and down. Anne-Marie screamed again, knowing that her death was on her, and then let it all go; praying as she collapsed that pulling the mountain down on top of them would be enough.

Eleven
The Curse of Silver

Brainerd struggled to his feet, with Cheyanne's help. They all stared at the figure floating before them.

Suddenly Fallon said, "It ain't her. It's the old man. Look." The others gaped at him. "Aura," he added. "*Look*, damn it."

"Astute, Jonas." The woman smiled. Her decaying face made it something hideous. "I would not have thought you capable of discerning such subtleties when the golden power masks so much. You must have been more conscientious about your studies this last decade. You have learned a great deal."

"Quitting whiskey helped." Fallon glared at the hovering form. "Where's Anne-Marie, then? You killed her and took her place? What the hell's it all about, Zeke?"

"She killed me," the woman said. "Tried to, anyway. When I discovered she had been with the black man." A hiss of disgust. "But worse, she defiled herself when she chose him to take her virginity. I had been grooming her for a decade! She was to be for Azathoth!"

"Azathoth," Lisbet said. "We were right, then. You hope to free him... It. Whatever it is."

"He is everything." Again the hideous smile. "I had such hopes for you all. We would lead the movement, we would transform humankind itself. Leave mortality behind... to *become*. Become something higher and better."

"We can see you're higher." Fallon's drawl held contempt. "All floaty and what-all. But better? With all them sores? You look like buzzard meat."

"Yes, exactly." This was Lisbet. She stepped forward, her tone full of urgency. For a moment she hesitated, then plunged ahead. "Ezekiel... whatever you are now... you are sick. Let us help you. We should have offered to do so long before. I should have spoken up to you ten years ago and I shall regret that always. But we can help you now." She took a deep breath, then went on firmly, "You must see this is madness. Look at what you have become. Your flesh itself is rotting. I cannot see how you are animate; at least in medical terms, that body looks as though it has been deteriorating for weeks. How are you even alive at all? After ten years? After the cliffs themselves collapsed on you?"

"Anne-Marie learned well," the dead woman said. "In her effort to stop me... she stopped *everything*. Time itself," she added. "Even as you learned the Language to shape the energies of the earth, she had discovered how to shape the flow of time. We were frozen in the moment of her death, her scream an endless echo of agony as her soul left her." She shook her head and then smiled the horrible smile. "It has taken these ten years gone to struggle free of the trap she laid for me. But once again the clock moves forward... and so do I."

"Then she really is dead." Aaron's voice shook a little and Cheyanne thought she had never seen such grief on a human face. He must have been hoping, even now, even looking at Anne-Marie's grinning corpse floating over them all, that somehow he could save her.

"Mostly, I think. There are still echoes." The woman shook her head, almost as though there were flies buzzing around it. Then she smiled again. "More of them, now that you are here. She must have reached out to you all. The silver marking you shows her call. It is a new phenomenon to me," she admitted. "But her aura overlays all of yours. She clearly sought your aid, at the end. And her power was such that even after all these years, you can still hear her cry. The beautiful thing about it is that I can feel her as well. When we merged, I knew what she knew. Her memories are mine now, and though her link to you, I know all about all of you as well. Your loves and your fears... and your betrayal." The smile faded to anger. "The little strumpet was plotting against me all along, it seems."

"Whatever." Brainerd had recovered enough to stand and speak again. "I just know that you herded us here with your birds and coyotes. Why? What's it all about?"

"What else?" The dead woman spread her hands. "I must say, you're not terribly intelligent; I was polite about it back then but clearly you are the same dumb animal you were when you first came to us, Nels. What could it possibly be other than finishing what we started ten years ago?"

"Uh-huh. I figured it was some silly shit like that." Brainerd hawked and spat. "Well, forget it. I ain't helping you do squat. Nor are any of the others. We ain't *with* you, don't you get it? It's done! You and the girl are *dead*! You just don't have the sense to lie down!" Abruptly his hands leaped into the air, as did Fallon's and Lisbet's.

Cheyanne realized that Brainerd had been trying to distract the dead woman long enough for the others for form a Hermetic link of some kind. A golden arc of energy leaped between Brainerd and the others and then coiled like a snake and flung itself at the figure floating before them all. Cheyanne flinched as the bolt scorched past her not two feet from where she stood with a thunderous boom of displaced air.

To Cheyanne's horror, the dead woman just chortled as the bolt splashed off her form and dissipated. "Really?" the figure said, and waved a hand.

Instantly a yellow-green cloud of energy enveloped them all, stopping them from moving. Even breathing was difficult; Cheyanne realized her chest was very nearly incapable of expanding enough to inhale properly.

The floating figure sniffed. "Trying to match power with me? You must be delusional. I have been studying Hermetics since before most of you were born. And I have had the last ten years to commune with the obsidian, to touch the souls of Azathoth and the others held there. Time means nothing to them. Nor to me, any more. You are insects, fleeting and trivial."

"Then why… are we… here?" Fallon was gasping as well, but still got the words out. "If we're so… meaningless."

"You are here because the girl called to you. I explained. But when I sensed you coming, I realized you were bringing me a gift." The green glow from the dead woman's eyes flared in triumph. She nodded at Cheyanne. "Azathoth's new vessel. Kuyagah, and pure."

• • •

The dead woman floated into the cave, still holding them helpless in the yellow-green energy sphere, towing them behind her as a child might tow a toy balloon by the string. "I know the history of the obsidian now," she said. Though her appearance was deathly pale and decaying, her tone of voice was sprightly, full of cheerful eagerness to share interesting facts. Like a schoolmarm, Cheyanne thought. Or a librarian, maybe. "Long ago, roughly the ninth century A.D. or thereabouts, an Arab sailor and his crew found the obsidian on an island in what we know today as the South China Sea. It was being attended by a group of mages who had cultivated the beings living within it, beings who traded the mages the gift of power for the sacrificial life force the obsidian needed to reach into our world from theirs. But the mages were crafty. They never gave Azathoth and his brethren what they truly needed to be free, but doled it out in dribs and drabs every seven years or so, prolonging their bargain and their own lives, by centuries.

"Then they made a mistake. They had taken a crewman from the Arab's ship as a sacrifice. The Arab sailor and his crew, in an astounding display of shortsighted ignorance, followed them to the island to retrieve their shipmate and killed the mages. They thought they had shattered the obsidian as well, but the shards merely retreated into the earth, where it gathered itself. It was not fully restored, but it was a beginning. Eventually it resurfaced in eastern Oregon in the form you saw at Stonegarden, sensing in the Kuyagah the same aptitudes for communication through Hermetic power that the ancient mages of the China seas had shown centuries before. But the Kuyagah were superstitious and afraid, and instead chose to contain the obsidian within the runestones, charging the circle with a Hermetic containment that I was unable to break until the night of the fire." A snort. "It never occurred to me to just knock over the damned things, not until one was shattered in my battle with Anne-Marie. The rest fell into the earth with the two of us and the obsidian was buried again, until I was able to free myself a few weeks ago. I had Philip and Larry as acolytes still – soulless, hardly more than automatons really." The dead woman nodded at the red form of Lawrence. "Philip, after ten years, was worthless. But Lawrence still had Anne-Marie's hand on him. He could function, after a fashion. I sent him out to find you and he got as far as Aaron, but that was all the poor thing could manage." She shrugged. "No matter. You are here now."

"You will not take Cheyanne," Doctor Lisbet said, her voice tight and hard. "She is my daughter. I will die before I let her come to harm."

As terrified as she was, Cheyanne's heart leapt at hearing the word *daughter*. Doctor Lisbet had never said it out loud, not until now. If the Hermetic paralysis had not held her frozen in mid-air, she would have hugged Lisbet and wept, and never mind how much the doctor hated dramatic displays. As it was, she tried to show acknowledgement with her eyes, and was gratified to see Doctor Lisbet smile briefly back at her.

The dead woman snorted. "You speak as though you actually pose some sort of threat. It's almost endearing. And from Lisbet! Lisbet being maternal is more shocking than Jonas growing into a true adept. Willing to die, you say, like a mother bear protecting a cub? Well, if that's what you want, we can accommodate you." She raised a hand.

"No!" Cheyanne screamed. "Please! Don't hurt her—don't hurt any of them! I'll do whatever you want!"

"I know you will, honey." The voice coming out of the thing's mouth was gentle and sad. "You have no more say in it than Lisbet. But she's not really your mother, you know."

"My real mother's gone, but Doctor Lisbet... She—"

The dead woman waved it away. "Whatever. I am not really interested in whatever grubby tragedy landed you with the doctor. I need your heritage. You are Kuyagah. And virgin. That's what I care about. It's necessary to restore the bargain with Azathoth. And your father is necessary as well." She gestured again and Cheyanne fell to the sand.

For a moment Cheyanne just lay there, grateful to be able to breathe deeply again. Then she sat up. "I can't help you with that," she said. "I never knew my father. He was gone before I was born."

"You little fool, he's here right now." The dead woman's expression was torn between amusement and exasperation. "Mr. Brainerd isn't worth much, he has no aptitude for the Language at all... but he is almost an idiot savant in one area. He is expert at persuading women to sleep with him. One of them was your mother. In Hyacinth, wasn't it? A Kuyagah girl, working the saloon. If work is what one calls those duties."

The words shocked her out of being afraid. Cheyanne whirled and stared at Brainerd. "Is this true? Did you know?"

"Swear I didn't." The blond man looked horrified. "I just… there been a lot of girls. I hardly remember Hyacinth. I was drunk most of that week. I had no idea there was a child of mine out there. Swear to God, girl. I been… I done stuff I ain't proud of but I wouldn't a' run out on you. I didn't know."

"Oh spare us your whining, Nels. I am about to offer you godhood and you carry on like a guilty schoolboy over some native whore from sixteen years ago." The dead woman was impervious to the impact her news had on them. "Listen to me now, both of you. Azathoth and his brethren were thwarted, ages ago, because a mage's daughter betrayed her father. Over a common *sailor*," she added with venom. "So for the bargain for power to be renewed, we must undo that betrayal. A father must sacrifice a daughter's virtue to the obsidian. Ten years gone, I had thought that it would be me giving them Anne-Marie, but I had not sufficiently understood the language of the runes. After communing with the obsidian directly, though, I know now that it must be a true blood relationship."

She paused and smiled, and with a pass of her hand, Brainerd fell out of the glowing sphere to the sand as well. "So… here we have a father and a daughter. Your purity is not in question, my dear, your aura makes that obvious." Cheyanne flushed but the dead woman was still oblivious. She addressed Brainerd. "So what do you say, Nels? Be smart for once in your worthless life. Agree to give me the girl and be the first of the new legion of acolytes in the army Azathoth will raise as they finally join us here on Earth. You have tasted Hermetic power before. That was as nothing to what I offer you now. You can be a god walking the Earth, ruler of this planet at my left hand. The *planet*, Brainerd! All you have to do is agree to offer me a daughter you were blissfully unaware of. An ignorant little hillbilly girl you hardly know." She laughed. "Or you can all die. I have time… I am immortal, as are the dwellers in the obsidian. I can start over. I have centuries. You have moments. Decide."

Brainerd licked his lips and would not meet her eye, and Cheyanne suddenly realized he was genuinely considering the demon-thing's offer.

There was a rustle from the darkness beyond where they were facing each other. A glistening black mass coalesced from the blackness of the tunnel, creeping to where they stood.

The obsidian. No longer fragmented, it moved and roiled like a living thing, occasionally casting out a pseudopod veined with gold that it then absorbed back into itself.

"Well, Brainerd? Decide!" Impatience now.

Cheyanne looked at him, her eyes welling. "Please. If there is any humanity to you at all—"

"I'm sorry." Brainerd licked his lips again. "Truly. About all of it, kid." Then, finally, he looked straight at her.

The silver was gone from his eyes.

● ● ●

Souls are the color of silver.

When Anne-Marie felt her death upon her, when the obsidian beings combined with Ezekiel's essence to crush her soulself and displace her from her own body, she flung herself outward, fragmented and terrified, her shattered silver soul finding a hiding place in her fellow Stonegarden refugees, connecting all of them. Part went to Fallon, part to Lisbet, part to Brainerd, part to the inert red thing that used to be Larry. Silver soul fragments fled to deep within each of their own essences, lying dormant until circumstances called them forward.

Eventually time would restart for Ezekiel and the obsidian thing buried under the rock. Anne-Marie knew she had not killed them, any more than they had killed her. Eventually they would awaken. And again, they would try to unleash hell on earth.

When that happened, she must be ready to stop them. She would need power. Not only her own, but theirs as well. They had to come together so that her soul could be rewoven, the same as the shattered pieces of the obsidian. She would not live, not truly… but there would be enough of her to make a difference. It was too late for her, but maybe not for the rest of the world.

So Anne-Marie—what was left of her—called to them through the silver link she had forged with each one. *Find each other. Find me. Come back.*

And they had, obeying a compulsion none of them truly understood.

Her old friends—her family, really, the only one she had ever known— were together now, in the cave under the collapsed mountain cliff where Stonegarden had been. The fragments of her soulself she had given them were close enough and enough Hermetic power had returned to them, that it was now possible for her to merge the silver fragments of her being. She could feel herself again. She was almost awake.

● ● ●

Lisbet. Stop. Please. You must listen.

Still held by the dead woman's golden power, straining with everything she had to be free, Lisbet thought she must be hallucinating. But suddenly, before her, she saw Anne-Marie, silver and translucent. Her eyes flickered from the silver form to where the other, fleshly one floated between Brainerd and Cheyanne.

It's really me. You must listen. You have come this far… We must finish this.

The voice was not truly there but rather an echo in her thoughts, the same kind of Hermetic echo she experienced at Stonegarden. Lisbet did not speak aloud but answered in kind. *Very well. What must I do? How can we stop them?*

Surrender. Surrender to the silver. I can release you, even amplify you, but you must let me all the way in. You have fought this ever since Jonas came to you. Please. Stop fighting me. It is the girl's only chance.

Lisbet nodded, closed her eyes, and did her best to reach for the contact she shared with Fallon and the others.

It was different this time. Before there had been pain and screams. Now there was surety, purpose… and beneath that, love. The deep affection Anne-Marie had for them all came blazingly alive within her, and she felt it resonating with the others as well; Jonas, Aaron… even Brainerd. Larry suddenly looked up and smiled, then his eyes were black and empty and he collapsed, truly gone now.

Lisbet herself felt such power she almost laughed out loud with savage joy. The silver left her, it left all of them, and suddenly with a flare of white the sphere of power that held them popped out of existence like a soap bubble. They dropped to the sand and faced the dead woman.

Brainerd turned to face the dead woman as well. "Yeah, here's what I'm thinkin," he said. "I ain't givin' them the girl. I'm giving them you."

The dead woman spluttered and gestured at Brainerd. Nothing happened. Somehow, Lisbet knew, Anne-Marie was blocking her power.

Brainerd grinned, the same wolfish grin that had women dropping their knickers for him from Arizona to Alaska. "Let's dance, you little bitch." He dived at the dead woman and gathered her into his arms, holding her pinned. The two of them flared white with power.

The dead figure struggled mightily, but Brainerd just held her tighter. "If you won't lie down I will lay you down my own self," he gritted, and then staggered towards the rippling form of the obsidian. The dead woman made a sound somewhere between a scream and a snarl, and then Brainerd shoved the rotting form into the black mass. There was a throaty sound of pleasure from the obsidian, and then it whipped out a tentacle and pulled Brainerd in as well.

"Help me!" he shouted at the others, and both Fallon's and Lisbet's hands came up, flaring silver-white. But it was too late. They could see Brainerd's flesh turn red and his eyes empty, and then he was sucked into the black mass as well.

Suddenly Anne-Marie was before them, the real one, glowing silver-white. "Nels is still holding it," she said. "But I must go in after as well. And I'll need help." She paused. "From you," she added. "I cannot last alone. At least one of you must come with me. It is the only way."

"A sacrifice?" Lisbet's voice cracked. "After all we fought to prevent?"

"Not like that." The silver woman smiled, sadly. "I will not last much longer here myself. Already I can feel the tug of the places beyond this one. It must be now. We must hold this monstrous thing and the beings inside it away from humanity. There are no Kuyagah runestones this time, no leisure for Hermetic enchantments. We must go inside it and help Nels drive them back. I can feel him—he is still fighting—but he cannot keep it up by himself."

"I'll go." Aaron stepped forward. He smiled at Anne-Marie. "It's a way to be together, ain't it?"

"Hold up, Aaron." Fallon was not convinced. "Even if this crazy notion is true, that you two and Nels can just beat them things back to their den and wall em up... How can we sure it'll hold this time?"

The look Anne-Marie gave him was pitying, and infinitely sad. "You want a guarantee? There is none. But we can buy some time. Another century or two at least. Perhaps longer. As the mage's rebel daughter did millennia ago."

"My decision, Jonas." Aaron took her hand. "Let's go, honey."

"A moment." Anne-Marie moved to where Cheyanne stood, staring wide-eyed with awe. She reached up and touched the girl's cheek. "You have been the best of us," Anne-Marie told her. "Ezekiel wanted someone pure of body but I think you are pure of heart. We are family, and Lisbet named you daughter. You are daughter to all of us from Stonegarden, now.

When the time comes... you will be ready. Yes?" A brief candleflare of silver-white arced from her hand to Cheyanne's forehead.

Cheyanne blinked and nodded.

Satisfied, Anne-Marie stepped back to Aaron and took his hand. She said, "We are going to take it deep within the earth... when we do, it won't be happy. This cave will come crashing down." She turned and smiled at the others. "So run. Now." Then she turned back to Aaron and he nodded once.

The two of them dived, hand-in-hand, into the glistening puddle of black. This time the sound from the obsidian was not a throaty, gluttonous victory noise, but a violent shattering crackle, a sound that Cheyanne thought somehow was both breaking glass and a scream of fury.

There was a rumble and shudder from the cave walls. Fallon gathered the two women to him, and they sprinted for the cave entrance hand in hand, Fallon and Lisbet pulling Cheyanne between them.

Moments later they burst out into the desert night. The wolves were gone. They kept running. Another hundred yards or so further into the open desert, they felt a rumble from under the earth, and stopped to turn and look.

The small ridge over the cave they had just emerged from was cracking and collapsing, as though the bedrock it stood on no longer existed. It looked to Cheyanne a little like a cake falling in an oven when the cook messed up. The rumbling continued, and the cliff face broke and fell.

"Second time I've seen this place fall," Fallon said. "But no sinkhole this time. I guess we really done buried 'em for good."

"Yes." Lisbet sank to her knees in the sand and exhaled a long, shuddering breath. "So much death. So much misery. Aaron and Larry and Anne-Marie... and even poor mad Ezekiel himself."

Cheyanne moved toward her and embraced her, standing so Lisbet's head could rest on her chest, and then Lisbet was weeping.

Cheyanne just held her.

The ground stopped its rumbling and shaking. There was silence except for Lisbet's soft hiccupping sobs.

Finally Fallon said, awkwardly, "Going to be a long walk out of here without horses."

Cheyanne looked up and glared at him. She pursed her lips and whistled, once, twice. Then she made a little nickering sound and let out one more piercing whistle.

There were hoof-beats and then Isobel came trotting out from behind a tumble of rocks. Behind the little paint pony came Sultan, and Fallon's big bay Girl.

"See? You treat a horse nice and give her a name, it's just like family," Cheyanne told Fallon smugly. "Izzy always comes when I whistle like that."

For some reason this struck Lisbet as hilarious. She burst out laughing and stood up, then hugged Cheyanne to her one more time before letting her go and moving towards Sultan. Fallon let out a snort and shook his head.

Cheyanne frowned at the laughter. "Well, it's true."

"I'm certain sure it is," Fallon said dryly.

Lisbet mounted up and smiled wearily at the two of them. "Come on. I should like very much for us to be away from this cursed place. We can see well enough by the moonlight for a couple of hours' ride, at least. Let's start for home."

Epilogue

It took them a day's ride or so to reach Sanctuary Valley. Denny and Coretta received them gladly, and they stayed a week. When Denny asked about Aaron, Lisbet told them that Aaron had given his life to save the rest of them, and when Coretta saw how raw the loss still was for them all, she shushed Denny when he would have asked more. Then she said, "But what you all rode out to stop? It's done stopped now?"

Lisbet nodded.

"Well, then, that's all we need." She beckoned Denny to join her. "We can bed you folks down in the barn if you like. It's not much, but—"

"I think I would prefer open sky," Lisbet smiled. "We have been too enclosed of late."

Coretta nodded and had Eli gather some straw for them to spread the bedrolls on. The nights were getting cold and crisp, but they were comfortable enough.

No one questioned their right to stay, nor asked how long they would be there. The three of them were accepted as easily into the community as if they had been blood relations. (Actually *more* easily than genuine blood family would have accepted them, Fallon added with a wry smile.) They were content to spend their days helping with chores and sitting around the fire in the evenings.

It was a way to just *be*, Cheyanne thought. *It's what we need.*

Cheyanne also, hesitantly at first, asked Fallon and Lisbet to tell her a little more about Brainerd. "You looked into his mind," she said. "Did you see anything... did you see my mother? What they were like?"

Lisbet looked uncomfortable. "Not... that we saw. But we were not really searching... I don't know how to answer that."

Fallon raised an eyebrow at her, then said, "Kid deserves a better answer than that. Miss Cheyanne, your daddy was not a good man. Not for most of his life. Hush, Lisbet," he added when it looked like she was going to interject. "Let me finish. Look, the fact is Nels might have left a litter of kids from here to California. He never hung around with any of them women long enough to see if anything came of it. We saw that much when we lifted the lid on him out in Metolius country. He was not what you'd rightly call chivalrous. But what you got to hang on to was when he did find out you were his daughter, he did right by you. You seen what the power can do. Nels threw all that away for you. Think on that whenever you're inclined to wonder what kind of man he was. I surely will. I've said some terrible things about Nels, most of 'em to his face. I regret that now. He had sand. And he did the right thing."

Cheyanne nodded and smiled a little. It wasn't what she had hoped to hear, but it was all there was. It would have to do.

On the afternoon of the sixth day, Fallon told them he would be riding on. "Where will you go?" Lisbet wanted to know.

"Been thinking on that." Fallon shrugged, then smiled, vaguely embarrassed. "Hate to admit Zeke was right about anything, but I think I found me a knack for studyin. I was thinking I might sail for Europe. Look at some libraries. London. Rome."

Doctor Lisbet's eyes narrowed. "You are thinking about the obsidian?"

"Little bit," Fallon admitted. "Wouldn't hurt to learn me some history of Hermetic stuff. Remember, she said no guarantee." He shrugged and grinned. "And you ladies?"

"I have patients waiting in Hackett Creek," Lisbet said. "And Cheyanne—"

"Actually," Cheyanne put in, "I thought I might stay here."

It startled both Fallon and Lisbet. "Why?" Lisbet said, finally.

"Because... these folks, they're family too. And Aaron was going to start a school here. You always said a good education was where success starts, that's why you started a school back home at Hackett Creek," she added. "I'm not as learned as you are but I have my letters and I know math. And the biology you showed me, and the stuff about herbs. I can at least help Coretta to read her Bible. It was something Aaron promised." Cheyanne's chin jutted out in challenge. "I know I'm young but I can do this for them."

Fallon chuckled. "Damn, Lisbet. She really is your daughter."

"I know." Lisbet smiled ruefully. "They are my own words, I can't argue with them. But... I will miss you, you know. Come see me every so often, all right?"

"Of course I will. And you too," Cheyanne turned to Fallon. "You come see us both. We're family. Don't forget it."

"Yes, ma'am." Fallon's grin was sardonic, as always, but nevertheless his words held genuine affection.

And that was where they left it.

• • •

Years passed.

Then decades.

No one ever knew about the horror that almost emerged in the high desert of eastern Oregon, no one but the few who had faced it and turned it back. And even for them, as the long years went by and horses and wagons were replaced with trains and automobiles and the wood and dust of the western cities were supplanted with concrete and steel, it began to seem like a dream.

The nineteenth century became the twentieth. The world moved on.

One day in 1957, in the Siberian wastes, not far from Krasnoyarsk, two men in parkas moved slowly across the tundra. They were moving in a careful pattern, a military sweep search. But they did not appear to be looking for a person. They stared intently at the ground before them.

One of them knelt, then reached into a small cleft between two rocks. He pulled out a chunk of black glass veined with gold. He nodded at his companion.

The other man pulled out a walkie-talkie, and spoke a few words to the dispatcher in Russian. "Tell Dr. Dracov we found it."

• • •

In a nursing home in Burns, Oregon, the old, old woman suddenly sat up straight in her wheelchair. "It's back," she whispered.

Her eyes were silver.

AUTHOR'S POSTSCRIPT

This was a different kind of story for me and I hope you all enjoyed it. The genre of "weird western" has always been a favorite of mine, from the days of *The Wild Wild West* and *Billy the Kid Vs. Dracula* to today's *Westward Weird* and *Cowboys and Aliens*. It was a treat and a challenge to try my hand at one myself.

But this book is about more than that. It's also about my dear old friend Anne-Marie.

I met Anne-Marie when I was a freshman in college, in 1979. I was living with my girlfriend at the time, and Anne-Marie was living with her boyfriend, and we used to double-date often. We were full of dreams. I was writing a lot and doing 'zines and things like that, my girlfriend had just been accepted into a prestigious art school, Anne-Marie was doing various roles in our local Shakespeare-in-the-Park, and her boyfriend had just been cast in a major play at the Civic. We had the world by the tail.

Then my girlfriend and Anne-Marie's boyfriend decided they liked each other better than they liked either one of us and that ended the foursome. But it served to bond Anne-Marie and I together as fellow victims of betrayal, and we became good friends forever after. There was no romance to it; we were both too freshly-wounded for that. Instead, we became brother and sister.

I was trying to figure out what to do with my life and Anne-Marie was telling me I was too talented to waste my time in community college, I should join her at the special honors program at the University, I'd fit right in there. Her intercession got me in.

And it was true, I did fit right in. Because everyone there was damaged goods, one way or another. There was a lot of drinking and sleeping around and weird psycho-sexual games, all of it overseen by a professor who seemed to enjoy the constant drama swirling around the place. There was some attending of classes, but there was far more boozing at the campus bar, and a lot of drugs.

More than anything, it felt like being in a cult. And like most real-life cult stories, it ended badly.

Of the core group of us, maybe twelve or thirteen in all, four are dead; one from AIDS, another two from drug-related problems, and one from just general abuse of his health. At least five others ended up in rehab for one thing or another. I'm not naming the school, or even the city, because for all I know it might have turned into something quite respectable by now. This was over thirty years ago.

But back then, it was a snake pit. I was lucky: I managed to get clear of that place pretty early on and have been clean and sober since 1986, thank you very much. Sadly, it ate Anne-Marie alive. She found heroin and never really came all the way back from it, though there were periods —sometimes years at a time—when she really did manage to clean up, but it never lasted, and it broke her health. She finally passed away, sick and alone, a few years ago. But she was always the sister of my heart, we never lost touch in all those years except during the worst of her junkie interludes, and I still miss her. In between all the dope and sickness and crazy, she was one of my best friends and we laughed an awful lot—not the brittle drug-fueled laughter we had in college, but the kind of genuine laughter and fun you only have with friends you have known for years.

That's the background. Here is how the novel happened. From a letter I wrote to an old friend of mine, one of the other survivors of that time in the 1980s...

I woke up shaking a couple of nights ago from this crazy dream where Anne-Marie was actually going to sacrifice herself to open a Hellmouth in central Oregon and a bunch of us from the Program had to stop her except it was 1867 and we were all ninjas. Broken, ex-ninjas. In middle age. Like we are now really, except some of us have sort of mended... and the ninja part. Now, I don't claim divine inspiration or anything. This is because of watching *Dr. Strange* and then a bunch of episodes of *The Magnificent Seven* TV show (the one with Michael Biehn) and trying to figure out the rewrite on the novel, and also because we had dinner with an old friend from high school, who is another one like Anne-Marie that can't get sober but refuses to ever hit the problem head-on.

It was just a creepy, disturbing evening. He was like... *hollowed out* inside. The person that was my friend was gone. Instead there was this smirking guy, brittle, self-deprecating but full of ego, married four times and cheated on all of them including the current one. Alcoholic too smart to go to meetings. We made awkward small talk for a poisonous ninety minutes until I gave Julie the eye and we called an audible. He laughed about how he was a bad risk and a bad husband, like that's just his thing, you know, like some guys are good at golf. Julie thought he was mean. All I could think was, *the poor sad bastard.*

So I had all that in my head, wondering what it was about us that made so many of us such bad risks back in 1981. In particular thinking about Anne-Marie and what a waste her death and most of her adult life was, constantly trying to hang on to that one time when it was all working and she was the belle of the ball.

And then this crazy remix mashup dream. Other people, smarter people, would roll over and go back to sleep.

Me? I have been thinking this is the prequel to the novel and I should write this book first, and then thinking I should *really* write it, somehow tell the story of all of us that got broken or burned back then with addiction and desperation and sex and stupid, looking for something, anything, that would fix us. Find a way to do it in my wheelhouse, tell something that's an adventure, something Ron would publish. But still a story with real teeth, that's *about* something.

This was written to the real-life "Lisbet," another refugee from those days grateful to have made it out more or less safely. A writer herself, she not only loved the idea but graciously granted me permission to use her as a character in the story... as did "Cheyanne," a former student of mine whose idealism and compassion always stood out to me, both when she was in my class and today, as a grown woman in her twenties. She seemed like the perfect foil for the aging, wounded group from Stonegarden, and it was a way to have a viewpoint character for the readers. Others in this story were inspired by real folks I knew back then as well. (You might recognize the fellow described in the letter as one of the main inspirations for Brainerd.)

The story itself took shape almost instantly. I always knew where it started and where it ended, and really the only things that changed in the process of writing it were the various set pieces as our group of heroes find each other. Sometimes research added things—I had never heard of Oregon's Black Exclusion Laws until I started reading about the 1870s in places like Canyon City and the Sage Desert, so I incorporated that into the story; without that, I probably wouldn't have come up with Sanctuary Valley, which became an important part of the plot. For that matter, most of the named places in the story are real and were as I have described them to be, except for the aforementioned Sanctuary Valley, Hackett Creek, Hyacinth, and of course Stonegarden itself. And there is no such tribe as the Kuyagah, they are entirely my invention.

Although even the made-up things have some basis in reality. I can tell you that in my head, Stonegarden Abbey stood somewhere along the ridge of the canyon running between eastern Oregon's John Day Fossil Beds and the town of Fossil itself. My wife Julie and I were out that way on a road trip a few years ago, and it's a very pretty drive. (Coming from the Cascades, take Highway 26 east almost to Dayville, then go north on Route 19 to Fossil. A big part of 19 runs along the canyon wall, and it's breathtaking.) I've always thought that the eastern Oregon desert, especially the Painted Hills, was an eerie-looking place; a perfect setting for some sort of *noir* Western adventure. For some reason, Western writers never use that country as a place to set a story, so I finally did it myself.

So that's mostly where it all came from. I will add that the more devoted followers of my work—all four of you!—will recognize "the obsidian" from a previous Airship 27 story of mine, from volume six of our series *The New Voyages of Sinbad:* "Sinbad and the Mages of the Obsidian Shard." The Arab sailor Ezekiel speaks of with such anger is, in fact, Sinbad. If Marvel can do continuity, so can I.

And as a private joke between me and fellow *Star Trek* fan Chris Kohler, our Pulp Ark Award-winning illustrator, I put in silver eyes as an indicator of psychic power, because I thought it looked awesome back when it happened to Gary Lockwood and Sally Kellerman in "Where No Man Has Gone Before." I leave it to the more obsessed Wold Newton scholars among our readership to decide if there is a connection. I'm not that far gone. I just liked the visual.

Special thanks go to Chris for really digging in on this. I sent him chunks of photo reference on the Eastern Oregon desert country, on the real people that were the basis of Lisbet and Cheyanne and Anne-Marie, and even a picture of a coyote in Oregon's Sage Desert from 1910 that, somehow, someone managed to get a great shot of in the wild, despite the primitive photography equipment of the time. Chris and I have been talking about doing a project together since we were both just a couple of wide-eyed nerds at the San Diego Comic-Con back in 1999, and though we've been published in the same magazine, we never actually got to work *together* until now. For that matter, I've never gotten to truly collaborate with an illustrator until now, where I can take the time to explain what I see in my head and then the artist goes and does his best to draw it. Chris being my first experience with this was a bonus and I suspect it spoiled me for life. My wife Julie will tell you that I just about levitated with glee every time a new set of sketches came in, because Chris just NAILED it. Also, apart from being an award-winning talent he's a really good guy, a great friend, and a total pro. Publishers take note.

That's about all I've got, except to thank my beta reader crew: Anne Hawley, Gus Lindgren, Lorinda Adams, Ed Bosnar, Brekke Ferguson, Ellen Johanson, and Amity Wills, all of whom had helpful things to say. And of course my wife Julie, without whom I doubt I'd bother to even get out of bed in the morning, let alone write stories.

And thank *you*, dear reader, for checking out our stuff. There is one more tale left to be told of the obsidian, the final chapter that is hinted at in the epilogue. *Beach Blanket Armageddon*, the story of the evil Soviet scientist Dr. Dracov who is attempting to weaponize the obsidian so his country can win the Cold War, is actually the novel I was going to try and sell to Airship 27 before I ended up doing a dozen other stories for Cap'n Ron instead so he could decide if I could write or not. If you all like this one, there's one more coming.

Ironic footnote: I actually did the first draft of *Armageddon* in college, and one of the beta readers on it was Anne-Marie. Another was the real-life Lisbet. Full circle.

ABOUT OUR CREATORS

AUTHOR -

GREG HATCHER - has been writing for one outlet or another since 1992. He was a contributing editor at WITH magazine for over a decade and during that time was a three-time winner of the Higher Goals Award for children's writing; once for fiction and twice for non-fiction. After that he wrote a weekly column for ten years and change at Comic Book Resources, as one of the rotating features on the Comics Should Be Good! blog. Currently he has a weekly column at Atomic Junk Shop (www.atomicjunkshop.com.) He also teaches writing in the Young Authors classes offered as part of the YMCA's Seattle Afterschool Arts Program for students in the 6th through the 12th grade. A fan of pulp fiction ever since he discovered the Doc Savage paperback reprints from Bantam Books in the 1970s, he has contributed a number of action-adventure stories to various 'new pulp' anthologies in recent years. Likewise a lifelong mystery fan, he has also written Nero Wolfe pastiches for the *Wolfe Pack Gazette* and several Sherlock Holmes adventures for the Airship 27 *Consulting Detective* series. He lives in Burien, Washington, with his wife Julie, their cat Magdalene, and ten thousand books and comics.

INTERIOR ILLUSTRATOR –

CHRIS KOHLER - has spent most of his life obsessed with drawing comic books and comic art. He has a couple hundred sequential pages to his credit, including the long-form work "The Portland Underground" (a zombie outbreak story featuring tainted Portland craft beer as the vector.)

In addition to sequential work, the last ten years have been spent doing interior illustrations and a few covers for Van Plexico's just-completed Sentinels series of three novel trilogies - winning the 2016 Pulp Ark Award for Best Interior Illustrations for *The Dark Crusade*. He has also recently started working with Airship 27 Publishing illustrating other pulp genre novels, the first being R.A. Jones' *Comanche Blood*. Outside of illustration for published works, Chris keeps his inking hand in shape by doing commissions, or classic comic cover recreations. His more-or-less complete works can be seen at http://dalgoda7.deviantart.com.

COVER ARTIST -

ADAM BENET SHAW –Accomplished painter, illustrator, and comics creator, Adam has garnered acclaim across a number of artistic media. After completing studies at the Cleveland Institute of Art in Ohio, the Edinburgh College of Art in Scotland and Watts Atelier in California, Shaw was selected as an emerging American artist to watch by European gallery owners and exhibited in London, England. He has been featured in "New American Painting", selected multiple times for the Arkansas Art Center's Delta Exhibit, and shown at the prestigious "Red Clay Survey" at the Huntsville Museum of Art. His work has also been shown in over 50 group and solo shows in the US and internationally. His figurative paintings are a prominent part of a 140-foot mural entitled "The History of Cotton" at the National Cotton Exchange Museum, St. Jude's Children's Research Hospital, the National Contact Bridge Museum, and a treasured part of private and corporate collections. He has created storyboards for several motion pictures, including Paramount Pictures' film "Black Snake Moan" directed by Craig Brewer, stage design for operas and corporate events, and character illustrations for the gaming industry. His published graphic novel work includes the series "Dead In Memphis", "Bloodstream" for Image Comics, "David: The Illustrated Novel" from Shepherd King Publishing and "Harpe: America's First Serial Killers" from Cave-in-Rock Publishing. He shares his love of art through teaching and workshops at his studio in the Broad Avenue Arts District in Memphis. Recently he has been painting book covers for pulp publishers Pro Se Productions and Airship 27 Productions.

TERROR ON THE PLAINS

Former Union scouts and saddle tramps Durken and McAfee are more than satisfied with their lives as cattle-punchers for Homer Eldridge and his Triple Six ranch. But fate has other, more sinister and weird plans for the two cowpokes...

Writer Fred Adams, Jr. spins weird western tales that will have readers on their edge of their seats and jumping at shadows. Mixing a heady brew that is half H.P. Lovecraft and half Louis L'Amour, SIX-GUN TERRORS volumes one through three are creepy adventures not soon forgotten.